AMISH WIDOW'S STORY

EXPECTANT AMISH WIDOWS BOOK 14

SAMANTHA PRICE

AMISH ROMANCE

Copyright © 2017 by Samantha Price

All rights reserved.

No part of this book may be reproduced in any form or by any electronic or mechanical means, including information storage and retrieval systems, without written permission from the author, except for the use of brief quotations in a book review.

This is a work of fiction. Any names or characters, businesses or places, events or incidents, are fictitious. Any resemblance to actual persons, living or dead, or actual events is purely coincidental.

CHAPTER 1

Levi King ran a hand through his dark hair and huffed in agitation as he stared at his older brother.

"I don't know what's going on with you," Andrew said. "She's been married to Abraham for going on five years now."

"I know that." Levi sat on a bale of hay and took off his hat while his brother sat down on a covered tin of horse food. "When Miriam told me Hannah was expecting, that brought it all back again—the fact that she's gone and I'm never going to be her husband."

Andrew shook his head. "I was worried about you when Hannah married Abraham, but I thought you'd get over it."

Levi nodded. He had thought he'd get over it, too.

"You're still a mess. And you know why?"

Here it comes! "Why?" Levi asked.

"You thought you could bury yourself in your business and your work while life continued on around you."

"Jah. That way I'm too busy to think about anything." Levi sat there in silence as he listened to his brother lecture him once more. This was just what he needed—some good common sense from his older brother.

Andrew breathed out heavily. "If you'd asked her out as soon as Matthew Miller ran off with that *Englisch* girl you'd probably be married to Hannah right now. I was sure Hannah always liked you."

"Hey, how is that helping me, saying things like that?"

"It's helping you because if you know where you went wrong you won't repeat the same mistake in your future."

Levi fiddled with his hat, spinning it in circles. "The moment is gone. This is a mistake that … It just became … all became real, you know? She'll have a family. Do you know how hard it's been to see her all the time, knowing she's married to someone else?"

"Levi! You can't have thoughts like that about another man's wife! It's wrong and you know it."

"I struggle with that. I know you're right. I'm doing my best."

"You need to get married and have your own *fraa* and *familye*. The sooner you marry, the sooner you'll forget the feelings you hold for Hannah."

"The woman I wanted to have that *familye* with..." he trailed off. "Never mind." Levi shook his head and looked down at the cement floor of the barn.

"Tricia and I have met a woman who's visiting here and we think you'll really like her. Her name is Lizzy Weaver. She's asked Tricia's help in finding a husband. Maybe that's the answer for you."

That meant his brother and sister-in-law had been discussing him and his reason for being miserable. He wasn't happy about that, but it was decent of them to try to help him. "There's a place in my heart and that place has been taken. It was her, or no one."

"Brother, you're on dangerous ground. It's one thing to be single and content with it. But you know what the word says about coveting another man's wife."

Levi rubbed his forehead. "I struggle and I admit that I struggle. I know it's wrong to have these feelings for her."

"All I ask is that you meet this woman."

He took his eyes off the floor and stared at Andrew. "For what purpose?"

"Don't you want your own *familye* — *kinner*?"

"You know how I love kids. It would be *wunderbaar* if you and Tricia could move back to Lancaster County."

Andrew shook his head. "I've got the farm and Tricia's got her *mudder* here."

Levi knew that Tricia's mother helped with their five young children.

Waving his hands in the air to make his point,

Andrew continued, "You've got to face reality sometime. And I don't know why you didn't do it years ago, when she first married Abraham. You should've put her out of your mind back then."

"I did. I knew she was gone then, but finding out she's expecting has just reinforced that she and I will never happen. I guess it's my fault. I didn't let her know how I felt. I regret that now but I can't go back."

"Exactly! You have to move forward and if you don't want to be alone for the rest of your life, I suggest that you meet Lizzy. No pressure, just see what you think of her."

Slowly, Levi nodded. His brother had always given him good advice in the past. Maybe meeting this woman wouldn't be so bad.

"Good." Andrew finally smiled.

Levi knew he'd have to put Hannah out of his mind. "Will this woman leave here and come back with me if things work out well between us? I can't move here."

Andrew laughed. "That's a fast change in attitude."

"I'm being practical."

"She told us she'd move for love."

Levi nodded again. "Okay, I'll do what you suggest."

"You'll like her. She's very easy to get along with and easy on the eyes."

Deep in his heart Levi didn't know how he could ever have a relationship without comparing everything the woman said and did to Hannah. And that would be unfair to any woman.

"I'll have Tricia invite her for dinner tomorrow night." Andrew stood. "Now we've got some fencing to do down in the south paddock."

Levi blew out a deep breath, rose to his feet, ran a hand through his hair, and placed his hat back on his head. He was no stranger to hard work and he'd worked even harder these past years to take his mind off one special woman.

Andrew wagged a finger in his face. "No thinking about Hannah."

Levi sighed. "I'll do my best."

THE NEXT AFTERNOON when Levi and Andrew had finished working, they arrived back at the house to see a buggy.

"She's here now," Andrew said.

"Good. I'm happy to meet her," Levi said, surprising himself. He was looking forward to meeting someone who might give him a new beginning, a new start, and a new lease on life.

"That's the way," Andrew said, jumping down from the wagon. "Why don't you go inside and wash up and I'll finish up out here?"

Levi jumped down from the wagon. "Thanks, Brother."

Levi washed up in the mud-room at the back of the house. Tricia liked her house spotless and insisted the men change clothes and shoes, and wash up thoroughly, before they entered her pristine and spotless home. Even with five young children there was never a thing out of place. The young ones played on the floor on a large blanket and when they finished, all the toys went back into the box and the blanket was folded on top.

When Levi had washed and changed his clothes, he walked through the back door of the house. A few steps further and he saw two women sitting at the kitchen table drinking tea. One was his sister-in-law, Tricia, and the other woman was pretty with fair hair. When she turned her smiling face to him, he saw her eyes were light blue. His brother had been right, she was easy on the eyes.

Hannah was a tall slender woman with light brown hair that had some blonde streaks when she was in the sunlight, and her features were remarkable. He silently admonished himself when he found he'd already compared the two women before he'd even said hello. *This is a new start,* he reminded himself. He pushed Hannah out of his mind and stepped toward the woman who might possibly be his helpmeet.

Tricia sprang to her feet. "There you are. Levi, this is Lizzy Weaver."

Levi dipped his head, and smiled at the attractive young woman. "Hello, Lizzy, I'm pleased to meet you."

She stood and put out her hand to shake his. "Nice to meet you, Levi."

"Likewise," he said, feeling a little nervous and realizing he should have said something else.

"I've been hearing a lot about you," she said, fluttering her lashes.

He smiled. "Oh no, that's not good. Who was telling you about me?"

Lizzy giggled. "Don't worry, it was nothing bad. It was all good."

It pleased Levi to hear her laughter. He'd been living amidst a gloomy cloud for years, and a woman like her might be able to cause him to enjoy life again.

"Sit down, Levi, and I'll fix you a hot tea before dinner to warm you up." While Levi sat down at the table in the kitchen, Tricia continued, "Lizzy and I were having such a nice time talking together that the dinner is going to be a bit late, I'm afraid."

"It's my fault. Tricia says I talk too much." Lizzy giggled again.

"And you live nearby?" Levi asked her.

"I'm staying only a few miles away. I just moved here from Harts County."

"You're a long way from home."

"I'm staying with my *ant* and *onkel* for about six months, and then I might move on again."

Levi got the idea she might be traveling around to find a husband. Many of the young Amish did that when they were searching for a spouse — travel from community to community. That showed him that she was a woman of determination and strength. He liked that in a woman.

"And are you a farmer just like your *bruder,* Levi?" Lizzy asked.

"*Nee.* I have a business back home, just a small business." He liked the polite way she spoke and how she held his gaze.

"What kind of business?" she asked.

"I'm a saddler."

"You make saddles and reins, and things like that?"

"I do."

Tricia brought back a cup of tea to the table and placed it in front of Levi. "Lizzy does bookkeeping."

Lizzy nodded. "I do. I used to do the work for many businesses before I left home."

Levi thanked Tricia for the tea, and then asked Lizzy, "How do you occupy your days now that you're here?"

"I sew, and I help my aunt look after her *haus,* and then there's pie drives and sewing bees and quilting bees." She giggled. "I'm probably busier here than I was at home."

Levi found that he liked her company. She was pleasant, sociable, and if she was a bookkeeper that showed she was an industrious woman who had a level-head. She would make a good *fraa.* He wondered how she was with children.

"Where are the children?" Levi asked Tricia.

"The older ones are playing in the living room and the little ones, are asleep."

He stood up and looked around the corner into the living room and saw the children playing, and then he went back to the table. "I've never seen them playing so quietly."

"Lizzy has a way with children. She set Maizie, Lily, and David up with games, and then she put Milly and Stephen to sleep by singing to them."

Lizzy giggled. "I adore children."

Question answered, Levi thought. And the woman laughed a lot, and Levi knew he needed some different energy around him.

Once the dinner was ready, Levi watched as Lizzy organized David and Maizie on their small table and the younger two, Lily and Stephen in their highchairs, all while cradling Milly, the baby, in her arms.

That gave him a mental picture of what his life could be like with Lizzy looking after their *kinner*. He could come home to a cheerful house full of children and laughter, and with Lizzy as the one to raise his children, they would all be organized and well-behaved.

His brother had been right. He was glad he'd come to visit Tricia and Andrew. This vacation was solely so he could put Hannah out of his mind once and for all, and this was an excellent way to do it.

~

Later that night, Andrew and Levi stayed up to talk after Lizzy had gone back to her aunt and uncle's house and Tricia and the children had gone to bed.

"I think I saw a little bit of a spark between the two of you," Andrew said.

"I did find her pleasant company, and I think she would make a *gut fraa*. She was excellent with the children."

"See, what did I tell you?"

Levi managed a laugh. "If it's all right with you and Tricia, I think I might stay on a little longer. I'd like to get to know Lizzy better before I go back home."

"Good! Stay as long as you like."

"*Denke*. I'll have to make a phone call and organize some of my workers to do extra shifts to cover me."

"Do whatever you need to do. This is important. These next few days could change your whole life for the better."

"Do you think so?" Levi hoped his brother was right.

Andrew nodded. "I do."

So Levi stayed a few weeks longer, and every time he was in Lizzy's company he found himself happy and smiling. He wanted to hold onto that happiness.

Finally, Levi felt it was time. He had to make a decision. He would ask Lizzy to marry him, and he'd bring her back home. He'd inherited the family house as he'd told Lizzy, and had lived there by himself since his brother moved away and his sister had married. The house was large, too big for just him, but it would be perfect for a family.

On the day he chose to propose, he prepared a special day for the two of them. He planned a picnic by the water's edge where they could feed the ducks, leisurely eat and drink, and look into each other's eyes as they talked.

He collected Lizzy from her aunt and uncle's place. And as soon as she had sat in the seat beside him, she started talking and hadn't stopped. She looked beautiful as she sat next to him. The warm morning sun made the hair that framed her face that much lighter, and her eyes sparkled and danced with enthusiasm.

"You haven't said much today, Levi."

He glanced back at her. "I haven't had a chance to get a word in."

She giggled. "I'm sorry. I'm just excited for our day. It's nice to have a whole day together. I'm glad Andrew is giving you the day off."

"So am I. He needs my help, and I'm happy to give it to him while I'm here. I'll be gone soon."

"Don't say that. I'll miss you when you're gone. I'm so glad you came when you did. I was getting bored out of my mind. I know it's a big community here and everything, but there aren't many people my age. Not ones I feel that I fit in with, anyway."

He glanced over at her, pleased she was genuinely sad about him leaving. "You'll miss me?"

She slapped him playfully on his arm. "Of course, I'll miss you. Maybe I could visit you?"

"That might be a good idea."

Out of the corner of his eye, he could see her draw back. "Might be? I thought you'd be happy about me visiting you."

He glanced over at her again to see her disappointed expression. He didn't want to ruin his surprise. He planned to ask her over lunch while they were sharing the picnic, so he changed the subject as he fixed his eyes back onto the road ahead of him. "I like this time of year. Look how beautiful the sky is."

She folded her arms and slouched down in the seat. Seeing her body language he knew she wasn't happy and she wanted to be sure he knew it.

"I'm sure the sky is just the same as where you come from. Haven't we been enjoying each other's company, Levi?"

"*Jah*, I've had a lovely time with you. That's why I've taken this whole day to have the picnic with you."

"You don't have a special girl back home, do you?"

"If I did, I wouldn't dishonor her by spending time with you," Levi said.

"I'm sad because you'll be gone soon and I'll be stuck here in this place."

He was starting to see a different side of Lizzy, but he reminded himself no one was perfect and everybody had their off days. She might have had women's problems. He knew from what his brother said that there were certain days where he could say or do nothing right as far as Tricia was concerned. He had to give Lizzy the benefit of the doubt because she certainly hadn't been sulky or sullen before now.

"I've got a great day planned," he said.

"*Denke*, that's thoughtful of you, Levi," she said, sounding a little less sulky.

They stopped at the park by the water, and he was glad that there were no other people there; it was just the two of them. Tricia had been good enough to prepared him a lovely picnic basket with wine, cheese, fresh bread, and grapes. He hoped to woo Lizzy with lovely surroundings and good food, in the hopes that she would say yes to his marriage proposal.

He pulled the blanket and the picnic basket out of the back of the buggy. She plucked the blanket out of his arms and marched in front of him.

Jah, she was definitely having an off day.

She spread the blanket out over the grass under a tree by the waterside. And when he placed the basket down, she said, "Sit down."

He obeyed, and she took over spreading out the food, passing him a plate and a glass.

"How are you feeling today?" he asked.

"I was feeling fine before you said you were going home soon. Now I'm feeling pretty upset."

They were at the picnic spot, a beautiful spot by the

water, just like he'd imagined he would be when he proposed to her, so what was he waiting for? He cleared his throat. "Lizzy, there's something I've been meaning to ask you."

She placed everything down and looked into his eyes. "*Jah*, Levi?"

"I know we've only known each other for a very short time ..." When he saw her eyes grow wide, he knew that she knew he was going to propose. He shook his head. "I'm a little nervous."

"Don't be. What were you saying?"

"Lizzy, I know we haven't known each other for very long, but I've seen the kind of person you are. You're kind and caring. I've seen your strengths and your great virtue and I was wondering if you'd do me the honor of marrying me?"

A smile quickly spread across Lizzy's face, and she jumped up and squealed.

Levi winced as her screams pierced through his head.

"Do you mean it?" she asked.

"Of course I do." He felt he should stand up since she was standing. When he was on his feet, he repeated his question, "Lizzy, would you be my wife and come back to Lancaster County with me?"

"*Jah*, oh, *jah*. Of course I will."

He was delighted with her response, and then didn't know what to do next. Should he kiss her on the cheek? Shaking her hand was certainly a little too formal under the circumstances. He leaned over and gave her little hug and a pat on the back. She stood on her tiptoes and planted a kiss on his cheek and then giggled again.

He chuckled, and they sat back down. Levi was relieved that it was behind him.

Lizzy grinned as she pulled out more food from the basket. "I'm so excited I'm getting married. I just can't wait until I tell everybody. Will we get married here or back where you live?"

Levi rubbed his chin. He hadn't quite figured out all the details. "Well, I'd like to get married back home."

"That's fine with me."

"Good. I'll speak to the bishop when I get back, and I'm sure he'll organize a place for you to stay when you get there."

She pouted. "Wouldn't I go back with you when you leave?"

"I would have to organize things for your stay first, and that will be the first thing I do when I get home."

"*Jah,* husband," she said with a giggle. "Now I'll have to do everything you say, since you are the man now in charge of me." She giggled and then poured two glasses of wine and handed him one.

Levi sincerely hoped he was doing the right thing, and if not, it was too late to back out now. He'd given his word and he'd been raised to know that a man's word was a man's bond.

CHAPTER 2

Back in Lancaster County in Hannah's house.

When Hannah walked into the kitchen in the morning, she saw her best friend, Miriam, busy making breakfast. She pulled out a chair and sat down. "*Denke* for staying here, I don't know what I would've done without you."

"You'll never have to be without me, we're just like sisters."

"These last few days have been the worst of my life. And then I'm faced with all of his clothes and all of his belongings. I'm going to have to figure out what to do with all of that, soon."

"I'll help you bundle them up when you're ready. Then we can send them to a charity."

"*Denke*. I'd appreciate that. Half of me wants to keep

some things and then at other times I think I should get rid of everything. I just don't know what to do."

"You'll figure it out. There's no reason to be in a hurry, give yourself some time."

"I want to keep some things for the *boppli*. My *boppli* should have something from his or her *vadder*—some kind of keepsake." Hannah sighed and rubbed her eyes. "Maybe his bible." Everything was overwhelming. There were so many things to do—so many decisions to make.

"Did you sleep last night?"

Hannah shook her head, knowing she needed to keep calm and relaxed for her baby's sake. She put her hand over the slight rise of her tummy. "This was the very worst time for Abraham to die. We were starting to get along better, you know? He was so happy about the *boppli*. He said he was starting to think he'd never be a *vadder*."

Miriam put a plate of eggs in front of her. "Eat up; you'll feel better with some food in your stomach."

"Why did it happen like this, Miriam?"

"It's not for us to ask why. *Gott* wanted him home. It was as though He reached down from the sky and plucked him up to take him back with Him. The last time I heard of someone being killed by lightning was when I was a little girl."

"It's so sad. My *boppli* will never know him. And he was never a *vadder* just like he thought—never really a *vadder* if he can't hold his *boppli*." A tear trickled down her face and she quickly wiped it away.

"Don't be sad. *Gott* wouldn't be putting you through this if you couldn't handle it."

"I can't. I can't." Now her tears flowed. She wiped them with the back of her hand.

Miriam leaned over and put her arms around her. "Oh no, I hope I'm not saying the wrong things."

"*Nee*, you're not." Hannah tapped her friend's hand. "I'll feel better once the funeral's over."

Abraham's body was in the living room already. The funeral director had brought the coffin there for the customary viewing. Only there could be no actual 'viewing,' given the state of the body.

"Will Levi make it back here for the funeral?" Hannah asked, hoping to have her good friend there beside her.

Miriam sat down. "I haven't been able to get in contact with him. I've called Tricia and Andrew loads of times, but there's been no answer. I've sent a letter, but it won't get there until tomorrow at the soonest."

Hannah shook her head. Miriam had already told her that her brother, Levi, had extended his stay in Ohio. She would get through the day much better if Levi was there. There was something about him that always made her feel calm.

"When will he be back?" Hannah asked.

"I can't say. All he said was that he was staying there a little longer and he had to organize his workers here.

I don't think he'll be away too long. He never likes to stay away from home."

"And the ladies are bringing all the food? I feel dreadful, not being able to do anything."

"In your condition, no one expects you to do anything. Just get through the day, that's all you have to do."

"Just don't leave my side today, Miriam. Everyone thinks I'm strong, but I'm not. I wish *Mamm* and *Dat* were still around. Nothing's been the same since they've been gone." It was times like these she wished she'd had siblings. She'd grown up playing with the next-door neighbor children, Miriam, and her two older brothers, Levi and Andrew. They were her family now that everybody close to her had died.

Hannah looked at the plate in front of her and pushed a fork into the fluffy scrambled egg, forcing herself to eat one mouthful after the other. She thanked God again that she hadn't had one sick day during her pregnancy; that had truly been a blessing. Because Hannah was only in the early months, not everyone knew her condition and she preferred to keep things that way for a while yet.

After breakfast, Hannah readied herself to receive the hundreds of guests that would flow through the house prior to making the trip to the cemetery.

Her head grew dazed as people and more people rolled up in their buggies and meandered through the house offering their condolences and saying goodbye to Abraham their friend, neighbor, and brother in the Lord. Nothing seemed real. To Hannah, it was almost as though she was watching someone else's life play out—this was someone else's funeral and not her husband's.

When the time came to move to the cemetery, four men picked up the coffin and loaded it onto the special long buggy that carried the Amish coffins. The buggy headed off, followed by a long procession with Hannah being first as she traveled with Miriam and Stephen. Hannah clutched at the black cape that she had wrapped tightly around her neck and shoulders.

When she had agreed to marry Abraham, she'd known how much older he was, and that one day she would possibly be a young widow but she had expected that to be a long way into the future. When she was in her forties or fifties, she'd thought, certainly not in her mid twenties and with a child, their first child, on the way.

As soon as Hannah stepped down from the buggy, a cold shaft of wind blew across her and she pulled her black over bonnet on more firmly and tied the strings tightly. The sky was filled with rounded gray clouds, not even a speck of blue finding it's way through the blanket of gray. It was an eerie day, she thought, a gloomy day, a perfect day for a funeral.

With Stephen and Miriam either side of her she made her way to the grave. The bishop's wife, Ruth, hurried over to her and Stephen stepped aside, moving behind his wife.

"How are you, Hannah?" Ruth asked.

"As well as I can be, *denke*, Ruth."

"Let Bishop Joseph and me know if you need anything, anything at all."

"*Denke*, I will. Everyone's been so nice and helpful already."

"I'm staying with her for a few days," Miriam said.

Ruth gave a kindly smile. "That's best. And you've been keeping well now that you're expecting?"

"Remarkably well. *Gott* has blessed me with good health."

"Good to hear."

They had been the first people to reach the grave and Hannah stood there looking at the coffin with Ruth on one side and Miriam on the other. For years she'd regretted her marriage to Abraham and had to seek God's guidance and grace. With news of the baby coming, Abraham had softened somehow. She had believed that once the baby was born her household would run smoother and Abraham would be a good father, and maybe a kinder husband.

It had been her parents who'd suggested that she marry Abraham, a good friend of theirs because, they had told her, he'd be a steadfast husband and a reliable provider. This suggestion had come at the lowest point of her life when the man she had been dating, Matthew Miller, left the community for an *Englisch* girl. She'd cried for two weeks after she'd found out about Matthew. Figuring she was doomed and all hope of marriage gone, her parents had offered her hope when they suggested she marry Abraham, who was looking for a wife.

Marriage to him hadn't been as easy as Hannah thought it would be. Hannah had thought that once she was married that would be the end of her worries and she'd have a life of bliss. How wrong she'd been. And all the hard work she had done on her marriage relationship was for nothing, now that he'd been called home. It seemed unfair, too, that he would not even see his child.

She was jolted out of her melancholy thoughts by a soft shower of rain. It was something that gave Hannah a bit of pleasure. She loved the rain, and she felt that *Gott* might have sent it at that moment to give her a little consolation.

The bishop cleared his throat. "Let us begin." Bishop Joseph talked about the cycle of life, and how death would come to each one, and the importance of staying on the narrow path until God called us home. After he finished speaking, Hezekiah Yoder stepped forward and sang a hymn. Then another man closed in prayer. When they were finished, the rain shower ceased, too.

All Hannah wanted to do now was go home and be by herself, but her house wouldn't be quiet until later on that night. First she had to get through the hundreds of guests who were coming for the post-funeral meal. Two of the ladies had stayed back at her house to prepare the food and lay it out.

"Come on. Let's get you home," Miriam said.

Hannah nodded and then looked around the crowd hoping Levi might have arrived, but he wasn't anywhere to be seen. "Still no word from Levi?"

Miriam shook her head. "I tried to call him just before we left your *haus*. I'll call him again when we get back there. That's all I can do."

"I know. *Denke*."

CHAPTER 3

It was over dinner on the night Levi had proposed to Lizzy, and Andrew thought he heard the phone ring.

"Is that the phone?" Andrew asked.

"*Jah*, it is. Leave it go, please," Tricia said. "We're having dinner and if it's important they'll call back."

Andrew jumped to his feet. "It could be an emergency." He headed out the door, leaving his brother, his wife and their guest, Lizzy.

"I'm so excited to be getting married," Lizzy said as she looked adoringly at Levi.

"*Jah* that is good news," Tricia said.

"And I've never been to Lancaster County before and that will be my new home."

Tricia nodded. "Good."

"I can't wait to have my own home. What's your home like, Levi?"

"It was our parents' house and now it's mine. It's quite big."

"Do you own it or does the bank?" Lizzy asked.

Levi was surprised she would ask such a question, but she had every right to know. Perhaps it might have been better to ask him that in private. "I do. Andrew has moved here and my *schweschder* and her husband have a *haus* and they didn't need that one, so now it's mine. It's the *haus* I grew up in, that we three grew up in."

"And does it have a large garden?"

"It had a lovely garden when *Mamm* was still alive, but I'm afraid it's been let go. And it had a wonderful area for growing vegetables."

"I can soon get it back to where it used to be. I will have lots to keep me busy."

Levi was delighted that she was so excited, and he was pleased that his home would soon go back to the standards that his mother had left it, with her lovely garden restored. And soon he'd be able to eat produce from their own garden.

When Andrew walked back into the room all eyes were on him.

"Who was it?" Tricia asked.

As soon as Levi saw his brother's face he knew it was bad news. "What's happened?" Levi asked.

"It's Abraham Fisher."

Levi sprang to his feet, pushing out the chair from

underneath him and knocking it to the floor. "Is Hannah okay?"

"Hannah is fine. Abraham has been called home."

A stunned silence filled the room.

Lizzy began to wail and Levi frowned at her. "Did you know Abraham Fisher, Lizzy?"

She looked up at him with tears in her eyes. "No, I just cry whenever someone dies." She put both hands up to her face and sobbed.

Levi had to get out of the house and get some fresh air. "Sorry about the chair, Tricia," he mumbled when he picked it up before he dashed out into the night.

He had to get home to make sure Hannah was okay. She was alone and to have this happen when she was expecting... She would be distraught. He had to call her and speak with her. He dashed into the barn and picked up the phone.

A hand grabbed the phone from him. He turned and saw his brother.

"What are you doing, man?"

"I've got to make sure Hannah's okay."

"The funeral was today. The community would've rallied around her. There's nothing you can do and besides, Miriam is there. She's the one who called, and she's staying with Hannah for a few days."

Levi felt all strength leave his legs and he staggered to sit down on a nearby hay bale. He held his head in his hands. "I can't believe that this is happening. I should've been there at the funeral. She's my good friend, we've got this connection."

"You've got to forget her. She's having a child. Her husband's child."

"She needs me, Andrew."

Andrew pulled up another hay bale and sat in front of his brother. "You've got a lovely woman in there who you're about to marry. You're going to start a fresh new life together. If you and Hannah had been meant to be, things would've turned out differently."

"Maybe *Gott* is giving me another chance to be with Hannah. He's giving me a third chance because I ruined my first two. Hannah is free now with Abraham gone. I had two chances to be with her, and I hesitated on both of them. I'm not going to hesitate now. The last time I waited too long and the next thing I heard, she was getting married to Abraham. Don't you see, Andrew? *Gott* is giving me another chance. We're both free to marry each other. There's nothing blocking me or standing in my way."

"You're not thinking straight. What are you gonna do with that woman in there? Can you see how her face lights up when she talks about your lives together? She's excited about getting married."

"I see where you're coming from, but you've got to understand it's no good for Lizzy if I have feelings for another woman. I'd be doing her a disservice if I marry her knowing that my true love is free to marry again. Don't you see, she's free now—she's a free woman? I'm not going to lose this opportunity. I'm not!"

"Hannah is having another man's child. Do you really think you could feel the same and give that child the same love as you would give one of your own?"

"Of course! I could love any child that *Gott* gives me as though it was one of my own. I've got a lot of love to give." He put his hand over his heart. "I will marry Hannah and I will love that child as a special gift."

"I caution you, brother. You must listen to me because my years on you come with wisdom. And it's with this wisdom I tell you that I think God is showing you, with the timing of it all, that it wouldn't be the right decision. You've given your word that you will marry Lizzy. Doesn't your word mean anything to you?"

"My word is everything to me, but the stakes are high here. Lizzy can find someone else. She's young. I'll tell her what's happened."

"You're that confident that Hannah would marry you?"

"Well, I hope so."

"Hope? We can all hope anything we like. Hannah wouldn't be the same woman you knew years ago. She's been married for five years, and before that the pair of you weren't that close."

"That was my fault."

"Are you sure you haven't created a grand illusion that isn't based on truth? Hannah wouldn't have given you two thoughts in years."

Levi didn't like anything that his brother was saying and a huge knot formed in his stomach. "The last five years have been wretched for me knowing that Hannah was married to another man."

"You're being selfish. Life isn't about pleasing you, it's about pleasing others. The word says, in honor preferring one another."

"You're saying I should be unhappy and marry Lizzy?"

"If you stand by your word, God will bless your marriage to Lizzy. I can't see that God will bless you if you let that woman down. How do you think she will feel once you've told her you'll marry her and then you dump her and go off and marry someone else? You can't do it. Besides that, you don't even know if Hannah will ever return these feelings you have for her."

Levi thought for a moment. "I'd imagine Lizzy would feel pretty bad. I see what you mean. But it would be good for Hannah and the baby if I married her because then she would be so happy and I'd be happy. And the baby would have a *vadder*."

"At the expense of Lizzy's happiness?"

Levi hated hearing his brother's words, but he knew Andrew was right. The right thing to do was keep his word, marry Lizzy, and put her first rather than himself.

Andrew continued, "This life we have here is a

vapor and will soon disappear, but what we do here determines where we will spend eternity."

"I think you're being a little dramatic, Andrew. *Gott* is not going to turn his back if I decide against marrying Lizzy."

"Maybe not. The decision is yours to make. I hope I've brought up some things for you to think about. I want you to weigh up everything before you make your next move."

"*Denke*. I'll think things through thoroughly before I do another thing. First, though, I need to make a call to Hannah and offer my condolences and tell her I'll be home soon."

Andrew nodded. "I'll go inside and tell the women you'll be back soon to finish the meal."

CHAPTER 4

Just as the last buggy full of people headed down Hannah's driveway on the day of the funeral, she and Miriam heard the phone ringing from out in the barn.

"Could you get that, Miriam? I'm far too tired."

"Of course." Miriam hurried out of the house.

The phone had rung often over the last few days with people offering their sympathies and asking if Hannah needed anything done. Hannah also had a pile of correspondence to read and reply to.

When Miriam walked back into the living room, she was grinning from ear to ear.

"Good news?" Hannah asked.

"*Jah*, Levi is coming home. He said to tell you that he's sorry he missed the funeral and he's coming back as soon as he can." Miriam sat down on the couch next to her.

"That is good news. I'm looking forward to seeing him."

"You two always did have a special bond."

"*Jah,* we did."

Miriam said, "I always thought that the two of you might marry."

Hannah smiled. "At one point, so did I, but that was a long time ago. We were only teenagers and then we grew up. If only I hadn't gone on that buggy ride with Matthew ..."

"Now don't start thinking about things or people that will upset you."

"No, don't worry, all of that happened so long ago now that it doesn't upset me. Matthew wasn't the right man for me."

"*Gott* will find you the right man when you're ready to marry again. You're still young."

Hannah shook her head. "I can't think of that right now."

"Of course not. And neither should you think of anything but adjusting to life without Abraham and preparing to welcome your *boppli*. Everyone knows it's not easy for you."

Hannah shook her head. "It's not. It was such a shock. It would've been easier if he'd gradually grown ill and then got worse. He left the *haus* perfectly healthy and then I got the news that he was gone. It's just been a lot to take in. I just have so many questions and I don't think they'll ever be answered."

"Life's like that. We probably won't know everything until we're in *Gott's haus*. Perhaps then all our questions will be answered and we'll understand it all."

"*Denke* for staying here, but you should get home to Stephen. I'm okay here and the sooner I get used to being in the house by myself the better. I really needed you over these past days, Miriam, and I don't know what I would've done without you."

"Am I wearing out my welcome?"

Hannah smiled at her good friend. "You could never ever do that. I'll be okay from here on in."

"Are you sure?"

"*Jah*, and if I change my mind I'll come fetch you."

"You could come and stay at our place if that would help."

"This is still my home even though he isn't here anymore. And I'll have to make it a happy home for me and my *boppli*."

"You will. You'll make a *wunderbaar mudder*."

"*Denke*, and so will you one day."

"When the Lord wills it."

Miriam had been married for years and longed for a baby. It almost made Hannah feel guilty when she shared the news of her pregnancy with her friend. Although, Hannah also had waited a long time—five years—for her baby to come along.

"As soon as Levi comes home you'll both have to come for dinner," Miriam said.

"I'd like that," Hannah said.

"Not tomorrow night, but the night after. He'll be home by then."

"Really? That soon?"

Miriam nodded.

"I nearly forgot I've got... I've got an appointment with the midwife the day after tomorrow. She said with all the stress, I should make appointments more often."

"Then I should come with you."

"*Nee denke*. I need to get used to doing things on my own. It's not far and my horse needs the exercise."

CHAPTER 5

*L*evi walked outside the barn to see Andrew waiting there for him.

"There, happy now you spoke with her?" Andrew asked.

"It wasn't her. I spoke to Miriam. Hannah wasn't in any fit state to answer the phone."

"She's grieving. That's only normal. It'll take her some time to adjust. Miriam will help her wherever she can. The two of them have always been close."

"It was the four of us who were close if I remember correctly. We were always in the fields together and playing in the barn if it was cold or raining."

Andrew laughed. "That's not quite how I remember it. I was older than the rest of you, and thought your games were silly."

Levi slapped his brother on the shoulder. "*Denke* for

giving me guidance. You're still being bossy and telling me what to do even now at this age."

"It's a tough job but someone's gotta do it."

Levi chuckled. "I better get back in to see what my fiancée's doing."

"That's what I like to hear," Andrew said.

When they went back inside, Levi told them he was going home. He could see plainly that Lizzy wasn't happy that he was going to go home the very next day, and going without her.

"You two were gone for a long time," Lizzy said.

Levi looked at Andrew. "Didn't you tell them I was calling Hannah?"

"I did."

Levi said to Lizzy, "I called home to offer my condolences to Hannah."

Tricia said, "I will write to her. I say things much better when I write them down."

"I told Miriam I was coming home as soon as I could. I'll get on the bus tomorrow," Levi said.

"And me?" Lizzy asked even though Levi had said he'd send her a bus ticket when he'd gotten things ready for her.

"I need to find you a place to stay first."

"I think you should take me with you. It would be hard to explain to my *ant* and *onkel* that you proposed, and then left me here."

Levi tried to hide his embarrassment at having to have a conversation like this in front of his brother and his sister-in-law. He said in a quiet voice, "Do you want me to explain things to them for you?"

Her lips turned down at the corners. *"Nee!"*

"We have already spoken about this, Lizzy. There's no accommodation. I wouldn't know where you could stay."

"Well, what about your *schweschder*, Miriam?"

"My *bruder*-in-law is extending their *haus* and they're living amongst rubble at the moment. They don't have guest space. I couldn't allow you to stay there. As soon as I get back, I'll speak to the bishop and he'll arrange suitable accommodation for you."

"And at the same time you'll tell the bishop we're getting married and make a date for our wedding?"

"*Jah*, I'll tell him. It's a little early to make a date, isn't it? My good friend's husband has just died and I'd like to make certain she's okay before my mind is consumed with wedding plans." When he saw her pout, he added, "I'll also have to arrange further time off for a vacation for after our wedding."

"It sounds like it will be ages away."

He shook his head, wanting to see her smile again. "Not ages. I'll make a date for our wedding when I meet with the bishop."

That put a smile on Lizzy's face.

Levi hoped that his brother had given him the right advice. But then again, he knew that the right thing to do often seemed the hardest thing to do.

When Levi arrived back home he visited his sister's house first, wanting to hear news of Hannah before he went to see her.

Miriam ran out to meet him and flung her arms around him as soon as he stepped down from the buggy.

"Levi, how have you been? You look well."

"The extended vacation did me good. But I don't think I picked a very good time to leave. I should've been here for Hannah."

"I don't know how many calls I made to Tricia and Andrew's *haus* and they all went unanswered except for that last one."

"At least I'm here now. How's Hannah doing?"

"She's coming for dinner tonight. I told her you'd be here."

That was the best news Levi had heard in ages. "She'll be here, tonight?"

"*Jah.*" She pulled him into the house. "Stephen has come a long way with the renovations. You'll have to see everything. *Jah*, we've still only got one usable bedroom and one working bathroom, but everything's coming along."

"Good."

Levi couldn't bring himself to tell his sister that he was marrying a woman he'd only known for a few weeks. Now that he was home, the whole thing seemed ludicrous. The thought crossed his mind how easy it would be to end the relationship from afar, but his conscience wouldn't allow him to entertain that notion for too long. Lizzy now expected a husband, and rightly so because he'd given his word. His word had been given in haste, he now thought, but it still was his word.

"What time tonight?"

"Come at six or thereabouts."

"I can stop by Hannah's place and collect her on the way."

Miriam shook her head. "No need, Stephen's doing that."

"It's on the way. Tell Stephen I'll collect her."

"Are you sure?" Miriam asked.

"Positive. I'm looking forward to seeing her. I never should've gone away. I should've been here when all this happened to Abraham. I heard he was struck by lightning."

"That's right. He was burned to a crisp and barely recognizable. The coffin had to be closed."

"That's awful! And Hannah's health?"

"She's doing fine."

LEVI WAS DRIVING HOME from his sister's house when he saw a buggy at the side of the road. When he drew closer, he saw it was Hannah. His heart beat fast with excitement at seeing her again—the first time in many years they'd see each other as single people. Lizzy wasn't even in his mind at that moment.

He pulled his buggy off to the other side and secured his horse. "Hannah!" he ran across the road.

"Levi, you're back already."

She looked just as beautiful as ever, yet at the same time pale and vulnerable. *"Jah.* I'm so sorry to hear about Abraham."

She nodded. *"Denke."*

"I'm sorry I was away when it happened. I didn't hear about it until the day of his funeral." He looked at her horse. "What's going on here?"

"I think Blackie's lame. I didn't want to walk him too far if he was, so I was sitting here not knowing what to do."

"Have you just traveled a long distance?"

"Nee. I've just come back from Sally Lapp's *haus."*

Levi knew Sally Lapp was the midwife all the women in the community chose to have their babies with. "Oh. Is everything okay?"

Hannah nodded. "Everything's just fine."

"I'll take a look at Blackie. I'll unhitch him and walk him out and have you watch for a limp." Levi unhitched him and then walked him up the street. "How does he look?" he yelled back at Hannah.

"I think he looks okay. He seems to be favoring one of his legs, but I can't tell which one."

Levi turned around and led the horse back. "Could be a stone bruise or something. He doesn't seem too bad." He picked up one of Blackie's feet and used a stick to remove some mud so he could see better. "His shoes are nearly worn through. I'll follow you home and take his shoes off and then you'll need to call the blacksmith in a day or two."

"Okay, *denke*."

When they got back to Hannah's house, he took a tool out of the back of his buggy and removed the horse's shoes while Hannah looked on. "Where are you keeping him?" he asked.

"I was keeping him in the main paddock, but I can put him in the stall in the stable for now. That's got the adjoining paddock where he goes in the colder months."

"It's best if he goes there. You go inside. I'll put down the bedding in his stall. That'll be better for his feet if he's got an injury. I'm no expert, but he doesn't look bad to me."

"*Denke*, Levi."

Levi led him into the stable and filled the stall with straw. With Hannah in no fit state to clean the stable, he'd offer to call there every second day. When he walked back to the house, Hannah was waiting for him with a mug of hot coffee.

"*Denke*. This is just what I need." He took a sip and she sat on the porch seat.

"Take a seat."

He sat next to her. "Hannah, I'm so sorry I wasn't here. I know I've already said that, but I want to be here for you."

"You're here now. And it was something that couldn't be helped. You weren't to know."

"How are you—really?"

SHE LOOKED into his dark eyes. And felt as though she were home. She should have been with this man at the beginning and they should've married each other. As they sat there on the overcast gray day, she was sure that he felt it too. It seemed like they were the only two people in the world. Taking a moment, she put everything into her memory like taking a snapshot so she could remember that moment forever.

"I'm as good as I can be," she finally said.

She heard him exhale before he took another mouthful of coffee.

"*Denke* for coming to my rescue just now."

"Always. I'll come back and clean out Blackie's stall for you tomorrow. And we'll see each other tonight at Miriam's. Are you still going?"

"*Jah*. I am."

"I'll collect you."

"I think Miriam arranged for Stephen to do that."

He laughed. "I told Miriam I'd do it, so Stephen has been canceled."

"Oh." Hannah gave a little laugh. "I feel it's just so odd that Abraham has gone. He was here one minute and in an instant he was gone. It's hard to take it all in. He wasn't even sick or anything."

Levi nodded. "It must've been a nasty shock. I'm here though. Anything you want or need, just ask me."

"*Denke*, Levi. I'm glad you turned up when you did. I might be still sitting on the side of the road not knowing what to do."

He chuckled. "You would've figured it out. You've always been independent."

She sensed things were a little off between them and wondered if it was coming from him or her.

"*Denke* for the coffee. Now I'd better get home and wash up for dinner. I'll be back soon." He rose to his feet, smiled at her and headed to his buggy.

CHAPTER 6

Hannah was excited about seeing Levi again so soon for dinner. She often wondered what it would be like to be a single available woman, and had regretted allowing her parents to push her into the marriage with Abraham. But back then she'd been immature, and had thought being married solved all problems.

It had been a struggle being married to Abraham, a daily struggle. He wasn't a happy man to be around and they never saw eye-to-eye on anything. But they had both made the most of things. She dared to think that this might be another chance, just maybe, another chance for Levi and herself. What if they married?

Levi had been single all this time and had never even dated a woman. Could he have been secretly in love with her this whole time? Now they could finally be together. She dared not think any more thoughts like that. It was far too soon after Abraham's death, but she couldn't help her mind running away with her. Maybe it was the pregnancy hormones that urged her to look for a man to care for her and her unborn child. In her mind, the only man who could do that for her was Levi.

Hannah wanted to have a proper marriage before she took her last breath on this earth. A proper marriage where she loved and adored her husband, rather than struggling every day to make something work that never should've been.

She placed a hand over her stomach. If she married Levi, her baby would have a wonderful father. She knew how Levi loved children and she was sure he would love the child as his very own. Excited to see Levi again, she put on her best Sunday clothes. The dress was dark green, and her white apron and cap were made from lightweight sheer fabric with a slight sheen on its surface.

Before she put her cap on, she brushed out her long hair. It had only been cut once when she'd managed to get thistles in it when she'd been playing in the fields as a child. The only way her mother could get them out was to cut her hair. Hannah smiled as she recalled how she'd cried at having short hair like a boy. She was around the age where girls start wearing caps, and was pleased when her mother made her one that very night. In the morning, she wore a cap and no one saw her dreadful chopped-off boyish hair.

She now braided her hair into several sections before pinning it on her head and placing her cap over the top.

A little before six she waited for Levi and soon she saw his buggy coming toward her.

Hannah closed the front door behind her and went out to meet him.

He jumped down from the buggy. "How's Blackie?"

"I haven't checked on him."

"I'll stop by tomorrow and take a look. We should get going to Miriam's *haus*."

"*Jah*. I suppose we should." When they got down to the end of the driveway, Hannah asked, "How was your visit with Andrew?"

"Good. It was great to see all my nieces and nephews again. They're growing up so fast and this was the first time I'd seen the *boppli*."

"It's a shame they live so far away."

"He had to go there, really, because Tricia lived there and she desperately wanted to stay near her mother."

That remark didn't go unnoticed by Hannah. Any other man could've said that Andrew would've found a wife closer to home, but Levi was a man who understood about love, she was sure of that.

Levi had never mentioned that she was pregnant, but she knew that Miriam would've told him because Miriam and Levi were very close.

When Hannah sat down for dinner with her friends she felt a great sense of comfort and peace. Eventually, she would like to marry again, and what better husband for her and father for her child than Levi? The way he'd talked to her and looked at her, she thought he might still have feelings for her and was being respectful of her and waiting a proper amount of time after Abraham's death.

She couldn't let him know that she was open to a second marriage, not this close after her husband's death. A suitable time would have to pass so she wouldn't look like she was jumping from one husband to another. The last thing she wanted was to be the subject of gossip.

"Andrew said you have a surprise for us, Levi?" Miriam said.

The three of them at the table turned to look at Levi.

"I can't think what that could be." He leaned over and helped himself to more potato salad.

"It sounded important," Miriam said.

"Nee, he must be having a joke with you."

"You know how serious Andrew is? He doesn't joke about anything."

Hannah gave a little laugh. "He is rather serious."

"How are the renovations?" Levi asked Stephen. "They look like they're coming along quickly."

"They are. I'll show you after dinner. I've got my

brothers coming to help me on the weekend and then we'll be just about done except for the roof."

"Sounds good."

Hannah worried about what the news could be. She feared that he might have plans of moving to Ohio. She couldn't bear to lose him. "You're not moving, are you, Levi?"

He smiled at Hannah. "*Nee,* I couldn't if I wanted to. I've got my *familye haus* here, and my sister and the business, and you to watch over."

Hannah smiled and looked down at her plate of food. She was happy that he was staying put.

"You've gotten so secretive in your old age, Levi," Miriam said.

"My life is an open book. I don't know what you're talking about."

"If Levi has something to tell us, he'll tell us when he is good and ready," Stephen said.

"*Denke,* Stephen. I knew you were a good match for my *schweschder.*"

"I can't win with the two of you. Speak up for me, Hannah," Miriam said.

"*Ach nee,* I'm keeping out of this one. I've learned long ago not to come between *bruder* and *schweschder.*"

When they finished the meal, Hannah stayed in the kitchen helping Miriam while the men went to the living room.

"He's got something on his mind, I can tell," Miriam whispered to Hannah.

Hannah wondered if it could be that he had her on his mind. That would be the best thing that she could hope for.

"What do you think it is?" Hannah whispered back.

"I don't know. But I'll find out soon. He's never been able to keep a secret."

Hannah winced. "I wouldn't say that."

"He can probably keep other people's secrets, but not his own."

"That might be right," Hannah said. When they had washed up the dishes and cleaned the kitchen, they brought coffee and cookies out to the men and sat down with them.

"I know I've said it before, Hannah, but I would've liked to have been there for the funeral. I picked a bad time to go away."

Hannah shrugged her shoulders. "I guess things turn out how they're meant to."

"You're like my *schweschder* and I feel I need to protect you, especially now that Abraham's gone."

"Miriam and I are here too," Stephen said.

"I'm very blessed to have you all." A tear trickled down her cheek. The reality was she was alone, and she didn't like that feeling.

Miriam moved closer, "Don't cry."

Hannah sniffed. "I'll be okay."

. . .

When Levi drove her home, he stopped outside her door and then before she got out, he said, "I need to tell you something, Hannah."

Hannah smiled. Was he going to hint at the fact he had feelings for her? Anything other than a hint would be too much too soon.

"*Jah*, Levi?"

"When I went to visit Andrew, I met a young lady."

All Hannah's hopes fell away. He'd met a woman and they were getting married. What a fool she'd been. It served her right for thinking about a man so soon after her husband had died and while she was carrying her late husband's child. She wanted to block her ears and run away.

Levi continued, "I asked her to marry me."

"Oh." Hannah looked up into the night sky at the twinkling stars and then looked back at him. "She said yes?"

He nodded.

"I'm sorry, that was a silly thing to say. Of course she would've said yes."

"I wanted to tell you first. Andrew knows and my sister-in-law, but I wanted you to be the first to know here. Miriam and Stephen have no idea. I'll have to tell them soon."

He didn't like her at all—it had been her imagination. And why would he like her? She felt she'd aged fifteen years in that five years of marriage and it must've showed on her weary features. It was only natural he'd want to start his married life with a young woman—she *was* probably young and fresh-faced, a woman who was quick-witted and also smart. She was no match for a woman like that. "I'm pleased for you."

"*Denke*. It's probably about time. I'm not getting younger."

"None of us are. Where is she from?" Hannah asked.

"Harts County, but she was staying with some people close by Andrew's *haus*. She's coming here soon to stay. I guess I'll have to look into that tomorrow."

"Things are moving quickly."

"*Jah*, I think that's best."

"*Jah. Denke* for driving me home, Levi." She got out of the buggy. "Good night."

"Good night, Hannah. I'm glad you're okay."

Hannah continued into the house and closed the door behind her, listening all the while to the clip-clop, clip-clop of horse's hooves as Levi's buggy continued back to the road.

She held in her tears and lit the gas lantern beside her and then she walked over to the couch and collapsed onto it. Now she felt truly alone. More alone than she had ever felt in her life. Her spark of hope had been snuffed out like the last candle in the darkest night.

CHAPTER 7

Hannah had cried herself to sleep right there on the couch. She couldn't bring herself to move into the bedroom. Climbing the stairs seemed way too much effort.

When she woke, she did her best to pull herself together for the sake of her baby. She washed her face and showered, and then she felt a little better. As she toasted some bread under the grill, she wondered what would become of her.

Her home was large and unencumbered, but she wouldn't be able to handle the land on her own. She'd have a talk with Stephen and Levi and see what they suggested she do. Abraham had left her with enough money so she wouldn't have to work for many years if she was careful, and that was before any money came in from farming. She thanked God that she had a solid roof over her head and money for her child and herself to live on. Things weren't that bad, she told herself.

She also had her friends, and soon she would be holding her sweet baby in her arms. Already she had so much love for the child that grew within her. Thinking of her baby brought a smile to her face. They would get through everything together.

Levi's news had left a hole in her heart, but Levi had never promised her anything. Not once had they ever expressed their feelings to one another although she knew in her heart that he had once loved her. But everyone changes with time and perhaps what had appealed to him about her in their youth was gone.

"But it just wasn't meant to be," she said out loud. Perhaps she could get a cat or two to keep her company. Abraham had never allowed cats around the place due to him being allergic. Hannah wondered if it wasn't that he just didn't like cats. Most people had cats in the barn to keep down the vermin. But a couple of house cats would be wonderful to keep her company in the coming days leading up to the birth.

She busied herself that day washing the curtains that hadn't been washed in many months. The busier she was, the less time she'd have to think about being alone. And when her baby arrived, she'd be plenty busy. By then Levi would be married and she'd be happy for him. He deserved happiness.

Just as she was sitting down for lunch, she heard a buggy. Immediately she hoped it was Levi coming to tell her that he'd changed his mind and he was no longer going to marry the young woman he'd met. Perhaps he was coming to tell her that he would marry her and take care of her and her baby. Then she remembered he'd said he'd stop by and check on Blackie.

She hurried to the window and looked out, and her heart sank through the floor when she saw Ruth, the bishop's wife heading to the house.

Hannah filled the teakettle with water and placed it on the stove, put her plate of food in the oven, and went to the door to meet her. All the while she was holding back the tears.

"How are you, Ruth?"

Ruth climbed down from the buggy. "I'm fine, *denke*, Hannah. I've come to see how you are."

"I suppose I'm doing as well as I can hope to be doing, under the circumstances."

Ruth nodded.

"Come in. I have the kettle on."

When they were sitting opposite each other, Ruth looked into Hannah's face. "Oh, Hannah, have you been crying?"

"I'm just so sad." The tears flowed, and she couldn't stop them.

Ruth patted her shoulder and moved her chair closer to Hannah's.

"I know it'll probably take you months to get over his death. Take comfort in knowing that he's in *Gott's haus*."

Hannah nodded. And felt bad for crying over Levi and never knowing how his arms would feel around her, never having him be the last person she spoke to at night before her head hit the pillow. Ruth would be horrified if she knew what was really upsetting her. "I'm just a bad, bad sinner," Hannah blurted out as she cried some more.

"We have all sinned. Not one of us is perfect. You couldn't have done anything different. When *Gott* calls someone home, they go home. Abraham is happy and at peace."

Hannah nodded but inside, Ruth's words made her feel worse.

"I'm sorry I'm crying."

When the kettle whistled, Ruth said, "You stay sitting and I'll make the tea."

"*Denke.*"

"You must feel so lonely in this house by yourself now."

"I do, it's very lonely, and this place is so big for just me. I suppose in a few months I'll have my little *boppli*. And I've been thinking of getting some cats."

"What a lovely idea."

"*Jah*. I think so. It'll give me some company."

"Do you feel that's what you need?"

"I do. I feel empty inside and two little kittens will make me happy, I think. Two little tabbie cats maybe. I don't really mind what color."

"Well, then I have good news for you."

"You know where I can get two cats from?" People often had kittens and puppies to give away to good homes.

Ruth's lips smiled so widely that vertical wrinkles formed in her cheeks. "*Nee.* I have something better than that."

"A puppy?"

Ruth laughed. "I have a young lady who needs a place to stay, and since you're lonely, it will be perfect."

That was the worst thing Hannah could imagine. She shook her head. "I couldn't have anybody staying here. *Nee,* I couldn't."

"You said yourself just now that you're lonely."

Hannah had a sneaking suspicion who this woman might be, and it would be her worst nightmare-come-true to have the woman who was to marry Levi staying with her. "Who is this woman?"

"It's the young woman Levi is going to marry. He said you and Miriam are two of the few people who know."

Hannah stared at Ruth wondering if she should make a confession and then decided against it. But it just wouldn't be right, her harboring feelings for Levi and having his fiancée stay there at the house. "I don't think I could have a guest. Thanks all the same, Ruth, but it just wouldn't work out."

"You can help each other. She'll be company for you, and I've already told her all about you. She knows you're a good friend of Levi's and she said she would do everything here to help you. And she said you wouldn't have to lift a finger. She'd do all the cooking and all the cleaning, and everything else for you."

"Oh, she sounds very kind and generous, but ..."

"That's settled then." Ruth nodded her head.

"*Nee*. But, Ruth, I didn't say ..."

"What is it, Hannah?"

"I would have to think about this some more. I don't want anyone here."

"There's no time to think about it, Hannah. She arrives tomorrow."

Hannah gulped and felt like she was going to be sick.

"Tomorrow?"

"*Jah,* tomorrow."

"I'm sure there's somewhere else she could stay that would be better suited."

"There's nowhere else for her to stay. As I said, you can both help each other." Ruth's attention was taken to something behind Hannah. "Mind if I have a cookie?"

"Oh, I'm sorry. I'm being so careless and not looking after you properly."

"I'll get it.' Ruth stood up and reached for the cookie jar and offered one to Hannah.

Hannah shook her head. "*Nee denke*." The last thing she felt like right now with her queasy stomach was a cookie.

All Hannah wanted to do was wallow in her self-pity. Being alone was the only thing she wanted now.

Having Levi's fiancée in her house would be like having a thorn in her side, a stone in her shoe, more thistles in her hair.

"You'll see this is just what you need. Someone to look after you."

AFTER RUTH HAD her fill of cookies and tea she left Hannah alone. Hannah had only a few precious hours, and then the very woman who had taken her last hope would invade her space.

Hannah scolded herself. The woman that Levi chose would be a wonderful woman, and perhaps the two of them could become friends. Hannah cheered herself up with that thought.

It was half an hour later that Miriam visited her.

"I just had Ruth here," Hannah said as Miriam came into her house.

"Let me guess. She wanted Lizzy to stay here?"

"Is that her name? She never told me her name."

Miriam nodded. "Lizzy Weaver. So you know that he's getting married?"

"He told me when he brought me home last night." Hannah hoped Miriam wouldn't see that she'd been crying.

"Are you okay with having someone live here with you?"

"*Jah*, it'll be fun."

"I suppose it will be company for you," Miriam said.

"Ruth said that Lizzy has offered to do everything around the place." Hannah gave a little giggle.

"Well, that's just what you need. You need to sit back and relax for a while and think about your *boppli*."

Hannah put her hand on her swelling stomach.

"What did the midwife say? I'm sorry I didn't even think to ask you last night."

"Everything's fine. Everything's going perfectly well."

"I know you're sad right now, Hannah, but you do have a lot to be grateful for."

"I know I do. I was just thinking the very same thing this morning. Sometimes we don't appreciate what we have until we lose it."

Miriam nodded. "That's right."

Hannah bit her lip. She'd had so many losses in the past few years. Now, she had to be happy for Levi and Lizzy. "*Jah*, I'm looking forward to her coming to stay with me."

"Good."

"She could become a good friend for us," Hannah said, forcing a smile.

"We can always do with more of those."

"*Jah*, we can."

"You know she's coming tomorrow?" Miriam asked.

"Everything is happening so quickly."

Miriam said, "I think Levi was a bit surprised because he was arranging her ticket, and then he found out that she'd bought her own. I think he was expecting her to come in a week or two or maybe three, and she surprised him by coming early."

"A nice surprise, I'm sure."

"*Jah.*" Miriam nodded and looked into the distance.

Miriam was still there when Levi came to check on Blackie, so Hannah couldn't talk to him alone. He cleaned out the stable for her and then told her to wait a few days before she called the blacksmith. Then he was gone, and minutes after, Miriam left too.

CHAPTER 8

The next day.

Hannah had been told that Lizzy was arriving at two o'clock. She had already made up one of the rooms for her and had prepared a nice meal in case she was hungry from her travels. It was ten minutes after two when the bishop and his wife came up her driveway toward her house. Hannah had done well, she thought, telling herself repeatedly that having someone stay there would be a good thing for her.

Hannah waited at the door and soon Ruth and a young lady were walking toward her while the bishop pulled various sized suitcases out of the back of the buggy.

"Hi, Hannah, this is Lizzy Weaver. Lizzy, this is Hannah Fisher."

"Pleased to meet you, Hannah. And *denke* for having me to stay at your lovely home."

"You're quite welcome. It's just me in this big place. I'm glad for some company."

Lizzy giggled loudly and Hannah thought she was nervous. She was a very pretty woman just like Hannah had suspected. Her eyes were blue, her complexion creamy and her hair was a pale golden-blonde color.

Looking over at all the bags Lizzy had brought with her, Hannah said, "Oh, you did bring quite a lot with you."

"I've got more at home and I'll get everything after Levi and I are married."

"*Jah*, good idea. Well, come inside and let's have a cup of hot tea."

"We can't stay, Hannah, Joseph has someone coming to the house to see him."

"I understand. Stop by another time."

"*Jah*. I will visit you two and see how you're getting along."

"We'll get on fine," Lizzy said with another giggle, and this time it was more high-pitched than the last one.

"*Jah*, I'm sure we will. I'll show you to your room, Lizzy."

The bishop carried all of Lizzy's bags up the stairs

and into her room, and after Bishop Joseph and Ruth left, the two women sat down for tea.

"I don't know why Levi couldn't have got me from the bus station. Do you know I had to get two buses and two taxis?"

"Well, it's quite a distance to come from Ohio."

"And that's exactly why Levi should've collected me rather than the bishop and his wife."

"I think it's because Levi's been away from his business for so long, and —"

"I'll soon find out. I'm seeing him tonight."

"Oh, is he coming here?"

Wrinkles formed in Lizzy's forehead. "Hasn't he arranged anything? I thought he'd want to see me on my first night here." Her lips turned down and she looked as though she was about to cry.

"I don't know. I haven't heard from him. Don't worry, I'm sure he'll stop by and say hello."

Lizzy sniffed and nodded. "I hope so, or this is not a very good start to the rest of our lives together."

"Don't worry, Levi is a very good man who'll do everything he can to keep you happy."

"I'm not happy now." She pouted, shaking her head rapidly.

"Cookie?" Hannah said, offering her the jar, and at a loss to know what to say or do.

"*Denke.*" Lizzy nibbled on a cookie while her eyes glazed over.

"I've made us a chicken casserole. Would you like some now? Have you eaten?"

"I ate before. A little while ago."

"We'll leave the chicken casserole for dinner, in that case."

"I intend to make myself useful while I'm here. Just let me know of any jobs that need doing."

"Just do something when you see something that needs doing," Hannah said, not wanting to have to give the young woman instructions.

"I heard your husband died."

"*Jah*, it was sudden. The funeral was just days ago."

"He must've been a very good friend of Levi's because he was so upset when he heard."

"*Jah*, Levi is a dear friend, to both me and my late husband."

Hannah was sure Lizzy had some lovely qualities and Levi must've seen them in her. She was still looking for what he'd seen.

"Ruth says you're having a baby, but you don't look like you are."

"*Jah*. I'm only a few months along and not showing very much." Hannah looked down at her midsection.

"I hope Levi and I have many *kinner*."

"That would be nice."

"But I suppose you'll only have one since your husband has died."

"Most likely, unless I marry again some day."

"*Jah,* many women marry a few years after their

husband dies." Lizzy wriggled in her chair. "What are we going to do tomorrow? I'm guessing Levi will be working since he isn't even going to make the effort to come to see me today."

"I hadn't given it much thought. Did you bring any sewing with you?"

"I can't sew all day. Maybe we can go shopping, or out to the markets."

"We could've but my horse has gone lame. He's got a stone bruise, we think."

"Does that matter?"

"*Jah*, I can't take him anywhere. He needs to heal." She pouted.

"I get quite a few visitors. Perhaps someone will visit us. Miriam will probably visit."

"*Jah*. I would like to meet her, but I imagined it would be Levi who introduced me to his *schweschder*. Can we call him?"

"I've got a phone in the barn. Feel free to use it anytime you like."

"Okay, I'll call him at work right now. He gave me the number."

Before Hannah could say anything, Lizzy jumped up and headed out to the barn. Hannah looked out the window at her striding purposefully toward the barn. That was one woman who knew what she wanted, and right now she wanted Levi's attention.

CHAPTER 9

*H*annah kept a watch on the barn and very soon Lizzy was marching back to the house.

When she came back into the kitchen, she told Hannah, "He said he can't stop by after work. I asked him to come for dinner, but he said he wouldn't impose on you."

"It wouldn't be imposing."

"That's what I told him. I thought I'd be spending more time with him when I got here." She slumped into a chair at the kitchen table.

Hannah sat beside her. "There's plenty of time; you've only just got here."

"I'm sorry, Hannah, you must think I'm awfully grumpy. I'm not like this normally. I'm just tired."

"That's understandable; you've had a long journey. I

expect you'll feel much better after a good night's sleep."

"I don't know when I'm going to see him. He said he'd call and collect me on Saturday morning. But that's four days away. What am I going to do with all that time? The bishop's wife said I should help you around here." She swiveled her head around to look at the kitchen. "The place looks clean enough. I don't see the point of scrubbing things and scrubbing things, day after day. Once a week is enough."

"I do a little bit every day and that way, the cleaning doesn't get away from me. It's surprising how much dust accumulates on things if you leave it too long."

Lizzy shook her head. "The bishop also said I should look after you, but you look perfectly fine. You're pregnant, not sick. Are you sick?"

"I'm fine. Perfectly fine."

"*Jah,* you look fine. They were making out you're an invalid that I had to look after. I'm not good at looking after people who are sick."

"When you become a mother you'll have sick children. They catch colds and things. You'll have to look after them."

"That will be different. I'll have to do that. And they'll be mine."

"My husband has just died, so I think Ruth thinks I'll be distressed and things like that."

"Will you?"

"Yeah, I go through ups and downs sometimes."

From what Lizzy was saying, she hadn't been the one to volunteer her help after all.

"Oh, Hannah. Couldn't we do something tomorrow?"

"Miriam will probably stop by to meet you."

"*Jah,* I have to make a good impression on her because she's my future *schweschder*-in-law."

"She's lovely; you'll really like her."

"Levi didn't tell me much about his family."

"Didn't he?"

"*Nee.* Could I have another cup of tea?"

"Of course." Hannah got up and poured her another cup.

~

HANNAH WOKE THE NEXT MORNING, and headed down to make breakfast.

It was ten o'clock when she went back upstairs and peeped into Lizzy's room to see her fast asleep.

She slowly walked back down the stairs and when her foot hit the last step, she heard a buggy. Hannah hoped it was Miriam and when she opened the front door she saw that it was.

"I'm glad you came, since we can't go anywhere at the moment," Hannah said when Miriam came into the house.

"Blackie still lame?"

"Jah. He won't be going anywhere for a while, Levi said."

"I forgot about that. Good thing I stopped by." Looking around, Miriam asked, "Where's your visitor?"

Hannah leaned in and whispered, "Still asleep."

"Is she sick or something?"

"I think she's just tired from the long journey from Ohio."

Miriam nodded.

"I'll make you a cup of tea."

Miriam followed Hannah into the kitchen. Just as they each had a cup of tea in front of them a bright and breezy Lizzy rushed into the kitchen smiling. When she saw Miriam, her face fell.

"Oh, I thought the buggy was Levi's."

Miriam stood up. "Lizzy, pleased to meet you. I'm Levi's *schweschder,* Miriam."

Lizzy smiled and shook her hand. "Hello, Miriam."

"Sit down, Lizzy, I'll get you a cup of tea."

As Lizzy sat, she said, "It's late. I'm sorry I slept so long, Hannah, but we had no plans for the day."

"Miriam has come to visit us like I thought she might."

"Wonderful," Lizzy said in a less than enthusiastic tone.

After Hannah made the tea, she was about to sit down when Lizzy spoke. "I haven't had breakfast yet. Could you make me some eggs, Hannah? I'm starving."

"*Jah,* of course. Would you like anything, Miriam?"

"*Nee denke.* I just ate at home."

Hannah set about making Lizzy some eggs while she listened to Miriam and Lizzy's conversation.

"I'm so pleased to meet you, Miriam. I had hoped that Levi would be the one to introduce us."

"He had more time off than he expected to spend in Ohio, so he's got a lot to catch up with."

Lizzy screwed up her nose. "He told me he has workers who help him."

"He does, but the more things he can do himself the more money he makes, rather than paying the wages."

Lizzy sipped her tea. "He's coming to collect me on Saturday and then he'll show me his house where we'll live."

"Good. It's a nice house; it's the one we grew up in. And Hannah used to live right next door, and the four of us used to play together. We'd go fishing, swimming, play ball games. We had a lot of fun." Miriam turned around. "Would you like some help there, Hannah?"

"No, I'm nearly done."

"I don't like my eggs runny, Hannah."

"Lizzy, do you know Hannah is expecting?"

"*Jah*, I know that."

"It's not really my place to say anything and normally I wouldn't, but I hope you don't expect Hannah to cook for you every morning?"

"It's okay, Miriam," Hannah said slightly embarrassed.

Lizzy drew her eyebrows together and pouted. "Of

course not. I'm here to help out. I'm sorry, Hannah. I just really wasn't thinking. I'll make all the breakfasts from now on."

"That's perfectly all right."

She put a plate of eggs and toast in front of Lizzy.

"I don't want us to get off on the wrong foot, Lizzy, but I'm just very protective of Hannah. Her husband has just died, and she's having a baby, so it's good that you're here to look after her."

"I thought I was here to … no one told me that's why they made me stay here. I don't mind helping out a bit, but I can't do everything. Even at my relations' place in Ohio I wasn't expected to do everything. I don't think that's fair."

Hannah sat down at the table. "No one expects you to do everything, Lizzy. I think you've misunderstood what Miriam said."

Lizzy raised her eyebrows and picked up her knife and fork. "Anyway, Miriam, now that you're here with a buggy and a horse that isn't lame, why don't the three of us go somewhere? Maybe to the stores? I hate staying home all the day long."

Miriam jerked her head to look at the clock on the wall. "Oh, look at the time. I just remembered there's somewhere I've got to be. I'll see you two later." Miriam pushed her chair out and moved away from the table.

"I'll see you out," Hannah said.

As she walked out of the kitchen toward the front

door, Miriam called out goodbye to Lizzy, who responded with something that sounded like a grunt.

Miriam and Hannah exchanged glances.

"I've started off on the wrong foot. I should've kept my mouth shut," Miriam whispered.

"Don't worry about it," Hannah said.

"Stop by on Saturday, since she'll be out with Levi."

Hannah nodded. "I will. Well, I'll see how my horse is. If he's completely recovered I'll stop by."

"If you don't show up I'll come here and bring something special for lunch."

"Sounds good."

Miriam hurried to her buggy and Hannah headed back into the kitchen to finish her tea.

As soon as Hannah sat down, Lizzy said, "She hates me."

"She doesn't. You just have to get used to her. She's very blunt and says exactly what she thinks."

"And she thinks I'm lazy, just because you made me breakfast this one time. I'm not lazy, I'm not."

"It's fine. Don't worry about it."

"Now what are we going to do today? With the whole day stretched before us. We could go to the markets."

"My horse is a little lame and I can't take him out yet. And he needs new shoes once his foot is better."

"Have you really only just got the one horse?"

"*Jah*, just the one."

Lizzy shook her head sending the strings of her

prayer *kapp* fluttering about her shoulders. "I hate it when I have to stay home and do nothing."

"We could rearrange things in the barn. I've been meaning to do that for some time." She still had Abraham's things to sort through, but she guessed Lizzy definitely wouldn't want to do that. And she wasn't ready to face it yet, especially with unwilling help.

Lizzy nodded and still looked unhappy.

Wanting her guest to have a pleasant visit, she said, "We could stop by the neighbors, the Beattie's. They're lovely people."

Lizzy smiled. "That sounds better than working in the dirty barn all day."

Hannah resisted pointing out that her barn wasn't dirty and kept quiet. "I just need to do a few things around here first, and then we can visit them in a couple of hours. How does that sound?"

"*Denke,* Hannah. I appreciate that. And I'll wash my own dishes. How's that?"

Hannah gave a little giggle. "Okay."

"And then you can tell Miriam when you see her next that I'm not lazy."

"Okay. I'll do that." Hannah was pleased that Lizzy was trying hard, and reminded herself that everyone had flaws.

CHAPTER 10

The Beatties' house was not far from Hannah's house, and Hannah pointed it out when she and Lizzy were at the front fence of the horse paddock.

"Are you okay to walk that far, Hannah?" Lizzy asked sweetly.

"*Jah*. The midwife said it was good for me to do a little walking."

They walked through the tall grass of the paddocks until they were at the Beattie's property.

"Are they old?" Lizzy whispered.

"About in their fifties, I'd say. They have one grown up son and he's moved away."

Hannah walked up the stairs of the porch with Lizzy close behind her. The door opened before Hannah knocked.

Mrs. Beattie stood there smiling. "Hannah, I'm so

pleased you've come. We were going to stop by and see you later today. We've got Joel coming back home to look after the farm."

"That's wonderful news. He's moving back to live here?"

"*Jah*, but we're giving him the *haus* and we're moving into the *grossdaddi haus*." Mrs. Beattie's eyes traveled to Lizzy.

"I'm so sorry. Where are my manners? This is Lizzy. She's staying with me for a while—Lizzy Weaver."

"Nice to meet you, Lizzy."

"Nice to meet you too, Mrs. Beattie."

"I'm Linda and my husband is Luke. Come in and meet him, Lizzy." They both walked into the house and the ladies all went into the living room where Luke was reading one of the Amish newspapers. He stood to greet them.

After Lizzy was introduced to Luke Beattie, he said, "Sit down, sit down. Both you young ladies should come for dinner tonight. Joel will be here by then."

"We'd love to," Lizzy said, speaking for both of them without thinking to ask Hannah first.

"*Jah, denke*. How is Joel?" Hannah asked.

Linda explained, "Coming back here will be good for him. He was about to get married and it was eight weeks before the wedding and the young woman just up and left the community."

Lizzy gasped. "That's terrible. The poor man. He must be devastated."

"He is. That's why he said a new start would do him good."

Lizzy nodded. "*Jah*, everyone needs a new start once in a while. My parents died a year ago and I miss them dreadfully."

"Oh, I'm sorry, Lizzy. I didn't know," Hannah said.

Lizzy looked across at her. "You didn't ask me anything about my *familye*."

Hannah hung her head while Luke and Linda offered Lizzy words of comfort.

After Lizzy thanked them for their kindness, she looked around. "Would you like some help around the place? I can see you've got boxes there, do you need them moved into the *grossdaddi haus?*"

"Oh, you're so kind, Lizzy. That would be lovely since Luke has a bad back and mine's not too good either."

Lizzy sprang to her feet. "I don't mind at all."

Hannah stood up too.

"You sit down, Hannah. You can't do anything in your condition," Linda said.

Hannah sat back down knowing Linda must've heard about her pregnancy. "I can do some small things."

"Nonsense."

"*Jah*, Linda and I will be just fine. Come along," Lizzy said. "You can show me where you'd like everything placed."

When they left Mr. Beattie chuckled. "It must be such a delight to have some company."

"*Jah*, it is. She only arrived yesterday and she's livened the place up already."

"Good."

Two hours later, they were walking back to Hannah's house.

"How did you like your outing?" Hannah asked Lizzy, half expecting her to grumble and groan about lifting boxes.

"What a lovely couple. I'm so happy to be going back there for the evening meal."

"*Jah*, they've been my neighbors for many years, ever since I moved into the house as a newlywed."

"It must be hard for you, now that your husband's died and soon you'll have a *boppli* to raise all by yourself."

"*Jah*, the timing wasn't ideal, I can tell you that."

"Where is all your *familye?*"

"My parents died a couple of years ago, and I never had any siblings."

"Your parents died just like mine," Lizzy said.

"*Jah*." Hannah nodded.

"And that's why you're so close with Miriam, because she grew up right next door to you?"

"*Jah*, that's right."

"Well, you can tell her how I helped the Beatties just so she'll know I'm not lazy. I wouldn't want her to tell Levi I'm lazy."

"Okay."

"I didn't want to tell the Beatties I'm here to marry Levi. It's proper if everyone hears it from the bishop when our wedding announcement is published. What do you think?"

"It's up to both of you—you and Levi—to do whatever you think is best."

CHAPTER 11

Right on dusk they were walking back to the Beattie's for dinner, and Lizzy looked over her shoulder back at Hannah's house. "Oh, what if Levi comes tonight to surprise me and we aren't home?"

"He would've said if he was coming. I don't think he'll do that."

"I hope not. It would be a shame to miss him."

When they knocked on the Beattie's door, Joel answered it. Joel was a little younger than Hannah and she guessed him to be around twenty two. In the three years he'd been gone, he'd become more stocky and muscular and Hannah thought he seemed taller.

He lunged forward and grabbed Hannah's hand. "Hannah, I'm so sorry. And I feel dreadful that I couldn't get back for Abraham's funeral."

"That's fine, I understand, and *denke*, Joel. I appreciate the sympathy."

When Hannah introduced Joel and Lizzy, she could tell by the sparkle in Lizzy's eyes that she was quite taken with him. The attraction seemed mutual.

The three of them sat on the couch and Joel explained that his parents would be out soon. Hannah guessed they might have been washing for dinner.

"It's lovely to meet you, Lizzy. And what brings you to this community?"

"The bishop and Ruth asked if I would look after Hannah, seeing her husband just died, and she's expecting a child."

"Hannah, I didn't know," Joel said. "That's such good news."

"It's only early days. Not many people know," Hannah said. "Your parents know, so I thought they might have mentioned it."

"No, they didn't. Don't worry, I'll keep it quiet." Joel looked back at Lizzy. "That's very kind of you, Lizzy, to stay with Hannah."

Lizzy smiled sweetly and gave a small giggle. "I'm sorry, Hannah. I hope I didn't give away any secrets. I didn't realize some people didn't know."

"Some do, some don't. News like this eventually gets around."

"And usually quite quickly," Joel said.

"And what do you do with your days, Lizzy, when you're not looking after Hannah?" Joel asked.

"I've just arrived here. I'd love to have a look around, but Hannah's horse is lame."

"Well, that's not, good. Would you allow me the honor of showing you around?" Joel asked with a smile.

This was the opportunity — the perfect opportunity for Lizzy to mention that she was engaged to marry Levi.

"*Jah*, I'd like that. But, I am busy on Saturday."

"Saturday's far away. I was thinking of perhaps tomorrow?" He looked at his mother and father who had just joined them, and they nodded in agreement.

"Perfect. I'd love that."

Hannah wasn't quite sure what was going on. It wasn't good for her to lead Joel on like that. Hannah wondered if she should mention the engagement, but it wasn't really her place. Lizzy was the one who should've mentioned it.

Throughout dinner, Lizzy was delightful. She listened politely, helped Linda serve and she even washed up afterward. Lizzy was the ideal dinner guest.

When Lizzy and Hannah were ready to go, Joel insisted he drive them home so they wouldn't walk through the fields in the darkness. When they arrived Hannah got out of the buggy, but Lizzy lingered there for a few extra minutes talking to Joel. When she came into the house and Joel had driven away, Hannah was waiting for her.

Hannah didn't want to be put in a position to have to tell Lizzy what to do, but she couldn't believe the way she'd acted toward Joel. "What was all that about, Lizzy?"

"What do you mean?"

"I noticed you didn't mention to any of them that you're to marry Levi. And you should've seen that Joel was interested in you. It's a recipe for disaster. And accepting his invitation like that—"

"But am I, though? Am I going to marry Levi? Where is he? If he cared about me enough, he would've collected me from the bus stop. And he hasn't been here all day. So am I engaged? You tell me." Lizzy stood there staring at Hannah with her hands on her hips.

"His sister explained that he was busy with work. He sometimes works about sixteen hours a day. I hope the Beatties aren't going to get mad at me when they find out. They're probably hopeful that Joel has met a nice young single woman."

Lizzy crossed her arms in front of her chest. "Levi needs to put me as his first priority."

"He's seeing you on Saturday, he said."

"That's what he *said*. Anyway, Saturday's a long way away."

"What about Joel?"

"I like him."

"That was more than obvious. But how is he going to feel when he finds out about Levi?"

"I'm not married yet. Perhaps I might like Joel better."

"Lizzy, the reason you're here — the only reason you're here is to marry Joel — I mean, Levi."

Lizzy giggled in a high-pitched tone. "See what you just said?"

"I just got the names mixed up."

"Perhaps you know in your heart that Joel is a better match for me than Levi."

"But you've only just known Joel for a few hours," Hannah said.

"Time will tell." And with that, Lizzy turned away from Hannah and marched up the stairs.

Hannah walked over and slumped onto the couch. This was putting her in an awkward position and it added extra stress. What was she to do? Should she say something to someone, or keep her mouth shut? She didn't want to say something to Levi because of her feelings for him. And that was exactly why she couldn't mention anything. Hopefully, things would sort themselves out.

CHAPTER 12

The next morning, Hannah woke to the smell of baking. She pulled on her robe and slippers and when she walked into the kitchen she saw Lizzy taking cakes out of the oven.

"*Gut mayrie,* Hannah. I've baked some cakes. I hope you don't mind."

"I don't. They smell simply divine."

"I've made an orange cake for Luke and Linda and a chocolate cake for Joel. He told me yesterday over dinner that he loves chocolate."

"What about Levi?"

"Saturday is days away. I can make him something on Friday. You sit down, Hannah and I'll make you breakfast."

Hannah pulled out a chair and sat down while doing her best to ignore the mess that spread from one end of the kitchen to the other. It seemed every pot and pan and every cooking ingredient was out on display.

"Oh, Hannah. I've used all the eggs for the cakes."

"That's okay. I'll just have cereal this morning."

"Oh, I'm sorry, Hannah. I've used all the milk too. I used the last drop in my coffee."

Hannah laughed, seeing the funny side. "I'll find myself some leftovers. Don't worry."

"I've already eaten. I ate before I cooked."

"What did you find to eat?"

"I had scrambled eggs. You really should get some chickens and then you'd never run out of eggs or have to go to the store."

"Perhaps you're right."

"So, that's another buggy horse, and chickens."

"*Jah,* it's all on the list inside my head," Hannah said, staring at the cakes cooling on the racks. "I'll call Miriam and ask her to take me to the store to collect some groceries."

Lizzy sat down. "I'm exhausted after making all those cakes. Would you make me a cup of coffee?"

"Sure." Hannah made Lizzy a cup of coffee and sat down with her once she'd made herself a hot cup of tea —black, of course, she thought with a wry smile.

"What do you know about Joel?" Lizzy asked.

"Lizzy, you're going to have to tell him you're engaged as soon as he arrives. Otherwise, people will get hurt."

"Hannah, Joel's just a friend."

"That's not what you said last night. You need to tell him."

"You're not my *mudder*, Hannah."

"I know, because if you were my *dochder* you'd know that you shouldn't do something like this."

Lizzy's lips turned down at the corners. "I can't cancel him. That would be rude. Anyway, it's my life. Just remember that. I'm not even certain if I am still engaged to Levi. He could've changed his mind for all I know."

"How about you wait until you talk with him before you see Joel again?"

Lizzy stood up and took hold of her mug of coffee. "I'm going to drink this on the porch. I think you and I need some time without speaking."

Hannah watched with her mouth open while Lizzy walked out of the room. She could see there was no point saying anything to Lizzy. She would have to do what she'd decided the night before, which was to keep out of things entirely and hope things would work themselves out. This was a matter for prayer.

Hannah heated some leftovers that she found in the gas-powered fridge, and when she finished breakfast, she set about cleaning up the kitchen.

Once she had gone upstairs to change out of her dressing gown and into some clothes for the day, she heard Lizzy back in the kitchen.

Wanting to keep out of her way, Hannah spent the next few hours sewing in her bedroom. She looked out the window when she heard a buggy and saw Joel coming to the house. The next thing she heard was the front door close. Lizzy hadn't even said goodbye to her, and she had no idea when to expect her back.

When Hannah went downstairs and back into the kitchen, she was confronted with another mess to clean. Hannah sighed, pushed up her sleeves, and began putting things back into cupboards.

Hannah had just finished tidying the kitchen and was on her way to the barn to call Miriam when she saw a buggy heading to the house. She looked closely to see that it was Levi.

CHAPTER 13

Now Hannah was in the very worst position possible. All she could do was stand there and answer questions, and she knew he'd ask where Lizzy was.

"Hello, Hannah," he said when he jumped down from the buggy.

"Hello, Levi. I'm afraid you just missed Lizzy."

His dark eyebrows drew together into a frown. "That's too bad. I arranged to have the morning off to spend with her. I'll take another look at Blackie and clean the stable while I'm here. I didn't think to tell her because I thought she'd be here. Where is she?"

"Joel Beattie was kind enough to offer to show her around."

"Joel's back already?"

"*Jah*. Lizzy and I had dinner at the Beattie's last night."

Levi rubbed the side of his face. "I heard some weeks back that Joel was getting married."

"Not anymore. It didn't happen. Now he's back to take over their farm. I was just about to call Miriam to see if she could take me to the store."

Hannah hoped that Levi wouldn't see how nervous she was. He didn't look too worried about Lizzy and Joel being together.

"I've got some free time, I guess. I can take you as soon as I check on Blackie."

Hannah shook her head. "No, that's all right. I'm sure Miriam could take me."

"I'm here. Let me take you."

"I couldn't," she repeated.

"How about I take you to Miriam's *haus* then?"

"*Denke*. I'll accept that offer. I'll just get my cape and watch what you do with Blackie." Hannah walked into the house and pulled her black cape off the peg by the door. She left the door unlocked just in case Lizzy arrived home first.

Levi led the horse outside to a soft grassy spot. He bathed Blackie's legs with Epsom salts and warm water. "I don't know what this does, but my *vadder* used to do this to our horses."

Hannah watched for the next twenty minutes as he bathed Blackie's hooves and legs in the warm water and salts. Then he carefully towel dried the horse's legs and placed him back in the stable.

"Are you ready to go?"

"*Jah,* but are you?"

He looked down at his wet clothes. "I've got a spare set of clothes in the buggy. I'll get changed in the barn and meet you back at the buggy."

"Okay." Hannah headed across the yard and waited for him in the buggy.

When he got into the buggy, Levi was laughing.

"What's so funny?" she asked.

"Girls and shopping. You probably plan to make a day of it and that's why you don't want me to take you."

"It's not that so much. It's just that I don't want to take up your time."

Levi stared at her. "You're acting a little distant today, Hannah. Is everything okay?"

"Everything's fine."

"Should I be worried about Joel and Lizzy?"

"In what way?"

He hit his head. "I'm such a fool. They're both single people who barely know each other. Does Joel know Lizzy is engaged to me?"

She was caught out and couldn't lie. Lowering her head and looking away from him, she said, "Not as far as I know."

"Hannah, how could you have allowed this to happen?"

"Me?"

Levi blew out a deep breath and turned his horse around to head back down the driveway.

Hannah wondered if she should tell him that she

told Lizzy to tell Joel she was engaged, but she decided against it because that might cause trouble for Lizzy.

"I'm not Lizzy's nursemaid. She's staying here at my *haus* and that's all. She's old enough to know right from wrong."

"I thought you and I were closer than that, Hannah."

Hannah knew he was angry and she couldn't blame him. "I think Lizzy feels like you're not making much of an effort and she was upset that you didn't collect her from the bus stop."

"Didn't you tell her I had arranged for other people to do all that because I was working?"

"*Jah*, I told her that."

He shook his head. After a tense journey, they arrived at Miriam's house.

"Thank you for driving me here, Levi."

"I'm sorry I took my temper out on you, Hannah. You don't deserve it. I just wish you would've said something to Joel and she wouldn't be out there with him right now."

"Maybe I should have. And now I'm sorry I didn't. It just kind of happened so fast."

Hannah walked to the house while Levi's buggy headed back to the road.

Miriam met Hannah at the door. "Come in. Was that Levi?"

"*Jah*." Hannah looked over her shoulder at his buggy, which was now a small speck on the road.

"I wonder why he didn't come in?"

Hannah shook her head. "He's upset with me."

Miriam smiled. "Upset with you? Come inside and tell me what you did."

"It was terrible, Miriam," Hannah said as she sat down. "We were asked to the Beattie's place for dinner because Joel came back. Joel and Lizzy hit it off immediately and now they're out together and he's showing her around the town."

"Are you serious?"

"I am." Hannah nodded. "And the other thing is that Lizzy hasn't told Joel she's engaged to Levi. I had a talk with her and told her that was the right thing to do."

"And what did she say?"

"She told me she wasn't sure if she was engaged to Levi because she hasn't seen him very much. Or, something like that. And then she got sulky with me and didn't even say goodbye when she left this morning. Of course, I couldn't tell Levi all of that, and now I'm sure Levi sees that it's all my fault." Hannah sighed. "I shouldn't be talking like this. I don't want to make trouble."

"That girl makes me so angry. She seems determined to get her own way with everything. She seems annoyed that Levi has to work all the time."

Hannah kept to herself how Lizzy had been acting in the house. That was information that Miriam could do without knowing, but as for the rest, Hannah felt much lighter having unburdened herself with what she had told Miriam.

"Anyway, enough about Lizzy. I came here to see if you would mind taking me to the store. I need some eggs and milk and a few other things."

"I've got a dozen eggs I can give you," Miriam said.

"Do you? That would be wonderful."

"I'm baking bread at the moment but we can go as soon as I get it out of the oven."

"*Denke.* I thought I could smell something nice."

"I don't know why Ruth thought to have that woman stay with you."

As Hannah followed Miriam into the kitchen she said, "It's certainly taken my mind off my own problems."

Miriam laughed. "That's something then. You'll have no time to think about yourself, but I do hope you'll get some rest while she's there."

"Me too. What is the date of the wedding?" Hannah pulled out a chair and sat down.

"No one's told me anything yet. I don't think a date's been set."

"Oh, I was hoping you might know something from Levi. Lizzy doesn't think a date's been arranged, either." Hannah sighed.

CHAPTER 14

Later that day when Hannah and Miriam were about to walk into the store, Hannah saw a buggy she was sure was Joel's.

"Look! I'm sure that's Joel's buggy. I wonder if they're having coffee in the shop there. Let's walk past and look in."

"Okay."

"You look in, Miriam, and see if you can see them, but don't appear to look too hard just in case they see you."

They walked by the window at a fast pace and when they were out of sight of the occupants of the coffee shop, Miriam said, "They were in there, and she was laughing."

"She's always laughing."

"I mean they looked close."

Hannah pressed her lips together, thinking how bad Levi would feel. "This isn't good. Do you think she'll end the engagement with Levi?" Hannah asked, now not wanting it to happen.

"I don't know, but I have to tell Levi about this right now."

"*Nee* don't. It will cause a lot of trouble."

"I have to, Hannah. He's my *bruder*."

Hannah shook her head hoping the backlash wouldn't come at her. Levi was already angry with her. "It could be innocent."

"They didn't look innocent, and you said she hasn't told him she's engaged."

"She might've by now."

Miriam glanced back at the coffee shop. "I can't imagine Joel knowing about her and Levi and still doing something like this, but I suppose we should give her the benefit of the doubt."

"I think we should," Hannah agreed.

"Let's just get what we came here for."

Hannah and Miriam headed into the supermarket.

When they were ready to leave, Miriam suddenly pulled Hannah back just as she was about to step out of the store. "Stop! There they are," Miriam said nodding her head toward them while she tugged Hannah's sleeve.

Hannah watched the couple walk to Joel's buggy. Lizzy looked happier than Hannah had seen her since she had arrived. Perhaps she was a better match for Joel.

Miriam said, "It sure doesn't look like she's told Joel anything."

"I'll ask her later when I see her at home." It was a conversation Hannah could do without.

"Joel wouldn't have taken her out for the day if he knew she was engaged. He just wouldn't."

"Just take me home will you, Miriam?"

"Sure."

They waited in the doorway of the store until Joel's buggy was out of sight before they left.

BACK AT HANNAH'S HOUSE, Miriam helped Hannah pack her groceries away. And then Miriam helped Hannah make a start on packing up Abraham's things, until Hannah suddenly felt overwhelmed. Miriam offered to do it all for her, but Hannah didn't want anything important tossed aside. Completing the task was put off to another day.

When Miriam left, Hannah pushed all her worries from her mind and settled down with pen and paper and a stack of letters to reply to. Abraham had so many relations—so many cousins. There were around twenty letters from people she didn't know, and around thirty other letters from people she knew, who had all been unable to attend the funeral.

Hannah decided to reread the letters so she could make a careful reply to each one and answer any questions that the senders might have asked. She pulled out the first letter and was halfway through reading it when she heard a buggy. Assuming it was Lizzy arriving home, she didn't get up to see who it was. When there was a knock on the door and there were no sounds of a buggy leaving, she knew it must've been someone other than Lizzy. She opened the door to see Levi standing there.

"Oh! Hello, Levi."

"I'm here to apologize to you, Hannah." He took off his hat and his gaze dropped to the ground. "I know you're not to blame and I took my anger and disappointment out on you."

"That's understandable. Apology accepted. I think you've already apologized to me, though."

She noticed he swallowed hard. "I've been so busy trying to get everything organized for Lizzy's visit that I'm afraid I have neglected her. Like you said."

Hannah was quick to point out that it wasn't she who had said that. She reminded him that she had merely been telling him how Lizzy had said she felt.

With the worst timing in the world, Joel's buggy approached the house.

"This is Joel and Lizzy now," Hannah said as they turned toward the approaching buggy.

Levi pushed his hat back on his head and walked

away from the house a few steps. He stood there with his arms crossed over his chest.

Hannah leaned against the doorpost, waiting to see what would happen.

Lizzy got out of the buggy and started walking toward Levi as though nothing was wrong, but before she reached him, Levi marched right past her to Joel.

When Lizzy saw Hannah standing at the door she went over to her. "What is he saying to Joel?"

Hannah shook her head. "I don't know."

"He wasn't supposed to be coming here until Saturday. Why the sudden change of plan? You didn't say anything to him, did you?"

"*Nee.* He rearranged his day so he could see you, and when he got here you weren't here." She bit her lip and then turned and looked at the two men who were engrossed in conversation. "You might have a choice to make, Lizzy," Hannah said.

"What? Between those two?"

"*Jah.*"

Lizzy looked back at Hannah. "I like both of them."

"It doesn't work like that. You can only have one."

Lizzy looked back at the men.

When Joel's buggy headed down the driveway, Lizzy walked over to Levi and Hannah slipped inside the house. She sat down again with her letters trying to keep out of things. But then she heard the raised voice.

"What did you say to him?" Lizzy hollered at Levi.

She didn't hear Levi's response, but then she heard

Lizzy's loud voice again. "You don't care about me. We're through," Lizzy screamed and then she marched straight into Hannah's house, slammed the door behind her, and then marched up the stairs.

Hannah froze, not knowing what to do. She hadn't wanted Levi to get married, but now she felt dreadful about the whole thing. Should she console Levi or just leave him be? She walked over to the door and opened it to see Levi's buggy leaving the yard.

Hannah sat back down and resumed her letter writing, trying to put everything else out of her mind—she was glad to have the distraction. When Hannah had just finished her third letter, she heard thumping. When she turned her head, she saw Lizzy stomping down the stairs.

"I'm going for a walk, Hannah. What time is dinner?"

"Um, around six?"

"I'll be back before then and I'll even help you with it."

"*Denke*." And then Lizzy was out the door before Hannah could ask where she was going, but she had a sneaking suspicion she was heading to the Beattie's *haus*.

A few minutes later, she was back.

"That was quick," Hannah said.

"I was going to find out from Joel what Levi said to him, but then I saw Levi's buggy at his *haus*. Now they'll both hate me. They'll be talking about me right now." She ran up the stairs again before Hannah could say anything.

Hannah was just about to walk upstairs to see if she could comfort her, but she stopped herself. She'd allow Lizzy a few moments alone and then she'd see how she was. *On to the next letter,* she thought.

CHAPTER 15

It was the worst idea possible that Lizzy was staying at Hannah's house. And he never should've asked her to marry him before he got to know her properly. Joel was shocked when Levi told him that he was engaged to Lizzy, and Joel had apologized to him and asked him to come back to the house to discuss things.

Levi had no idea what Joel wanted to discuss, but he was sure they could sort something out between them. What had happened was not right. The only thing he knew was that it had nothing to do with Hannah. He regretted the temper that sometimes overcame him out of nowhere. It was his major flaw.

If only he'd ignored Andrew telling him he needed a wife. Sure, he wanted a wife and a family, but what he didn't need were problems at this stage of his life. He knew now that he and Lizzy weren't suited, and if he were to ask Hannah to marry him anytime soon she would feel second best—second choice.

When he got out of the buggy, he walked over to Joel who was unhitching his horse from the buggy.

Joel straightened up. "As I said, Levi, she said nothing about being engaged to you."

"I believe it." Levi shook his head, feeling he'd been made a fool of, and it happened in front of Hannah. "I don't think Lizzy and I are suited. If we were, she wouldn't have accepted your invitation."

Joel shook his head. "I feel bad about this, Levi. Are you calling off the engagement?"

"I think I will have to have a talk with Lizzy and then we both have decisions to make."

Joel nodded. "I understand. I have to be honest with you, Levi, and tell you that if things don't work out between the two of you, I would like to see her again."

"Well, at least that would mean she hasn't come all this way for nothing."

"There would be no hard feelings?"

"If that's the outcome, then there'd be no hard feelings, but I do have to talk to Lizzy first."

"I understand."

"Anyway, Joel, it's good to see you home, my good friend"

"It's good to be back. I was meant to be getting married but that didn't work out and now my parents need me here, so here I am."

"I'll go back and talk to Lizzy now. There's no use allowing this to linger for a few days."

Joel nodded. "Understood. And I surely wouldn't have offered to show her around today if I had known you were engaged."

Levi nodded. "I know. I know."

The two men shook hands and then Levi headed back the short distance to Hannah's house.

He felt foolish that this was all playing out in front of Hannah, but there was nothing he could do about it now.

He knocked on Hannah's door and when she opened it she looked surprised to see him. "You're back."

"I am. I was wondering if I might speak to Lizzy?"

"Come in and take a seat in the living room. I'll tell her you're here."

"Okay, thanks." He settled himself down in the living room and looked at the pile of letters on the coffee table. Then he heard muffled voices above him, and Hannah came down the stairs alone.

"She'll be down in a minute," Hannah said.

Denke.

"Well, I've got some things I need to tend to in the barn, so I'll leave the two of you to it."

"Thanks again, Hannah." He was pleased that she would be well out of earshot when the conversation took place.

CHAPTER 16

Hannah walked into the barn and reminded herself to get those two kittens she'd been thinking about.

When she was a young girl she'd had three cats, but they had lived mostly in the barn. It seemed odd now to go into a barn and not see a cat or maybe two stretched out fast asleep.

This wasn't exactly where she'd seen herself in her mid-twenties—a widow with a baby on the way.

She sat down on the chair by the phone, waiting for Levi to finish speaking with Lizzy. Levi was ending the relationship by his tone of voice and the expression on his face. She knew him well.

Hannah closed her eyes and wondered how things would be different if she had just said no when Matthew Miller had asked her on a buggy ride all those years ago. It seemed like a lifetime ago. She'd decided at the time she couldn't wait for Levi forever. Life seemed so full of possibilities back then. Now, she knew how crucial it was to make the right decisions in one's youth.

She put her hand over her swollen belly. Why did life have to be so complicated sometimes? Things hadn't been straightforward for her in regard to relationships, and neither had they for Levi, it seemed.

Hannah stood up and peered through the partly open barn door and back toward the house. "I wonder if they've started talking yet?" She mumbled to herself. "Or, she could still be in the bedroom." Sitting back down she gave a deep sigh.

∼

Levi rose to his feet when he saw Lizzy walking down the stairs. His heart was flat when he saw her and he knew that if he were truly in love with her, or if they were meant to marry, he would've felt something inside. All he felt was confusion. He didn't know this woman at all, he realized, and neither could he work out what she'd been thinking to go off with Joel like she had today.

"You wanted to talk with me, Levi?"

"I do. Take a seat."

She sat opposite him. "If I'd known you were coming out today I wouldn't have gone with Joel."

"You went out with a single man and didn't tell him that you are engaged to me."

"No one knows we're engaged."

He couldn't work out what she was talking about. Was she trying to deflect what she'd done? "They do. The bishop and his wife, and so do all my *familye*."

"Does it really matter?" she asked.

"*Jah*, it does matter. Of course it matters."

"I don't want a husband who puts me last, Levi. And I think you're too involved in your work to have a *fraa*. A woman can't just live on cooking and cleaning and raising *kinner* alone. You've made me feel unwelcome. You hardly said two words to me on the phone when I called you."

"I was busy and had people all over the place, and orders to fill. I don't know what you think I'm supposed to do. If I'm going to be a good provider, I need to work."

"Perhaps I'd be better off with a farmer like Joel. He'd be close to the *haus* and he'd come home for the midday meal."

"Is that what you want?"

"*Jah*. That's exactly what I want. And I wish I'd never come here. You've made me feel so unwelcome." She blinked rapidly as though she was going to cry.

He stared at her and wondered why he'd listened to his brother. She had wanted to come early and that's why things weren't organized. "I was trying to fix things for you before you came here. If you had just waited a few weeks like I wanted, I would've had everything properly arranged by the time you got here."

"Are you making out it's my fault?"

He shook his head. "*Nee*. It's no one's fault. I'm just pointing out to you that I had no time to make you feel welcome and, had you waited, you would've felt welcome. I would've arranged somewhere for you to stay. I don't know that it's right for you to stay with Hannah after she's just lost her husband in such a tragic way."

"I don't want to fight with you, Levi. I don't like arguing."

"I don't want to argue either. It seems we are just two different people and we want two different things out of life. We're too dissimilar to be together."

"That's right. So this relationship is officially over."

He was relieved to hear it and glad she'd come to that conclusion rather than it be his decision, since she'd moved there for him. "*Jah*, if that's your decision it is over."

She bounded to her feet. "Well, goodbye." She marched back up the stairs while Levi watched open mouthed.

He blew out a deep breath. Now he had to go to the bishop and explain that the wedding was not going to take place. Hopefully, the bishop wouldn't ask too many probing questions on why the relationship hadn't worked. He did not want to bring Joel's name into it.

He walked into the barn to say goodbye to Hannah.

"Are you here, Hannah?"

Hannah stood. "*Jah*, I'm over here." She walked closer to the door. "Have you finished your talk?"

He shrugged. "We're finished talking, and you might as well know that the relationship is over."

"I'm sorry. That's too bad." She was genuinely sorry for him, although glad in another way because she didn't think they made a good pair.

"We weren't suited and it's better to find that out now, and not after we were married."

Hannah felt tears stinging behind her eyes and before she knew it the tears were flooding down her cheeks. It hurt her to think that Levi was sad.

"What's the matter?" he asked stepping closer.

"I don't know. It's just so sad. You thought you were getting married and now you aren't."

"Hey, stop crying. It happened to me not you."

She gave a little laugh and managed to make herself stop. "I've just had a lot of changes in my life and it's hard for me to get used to everything that's been going on."

"I know, I know. It must be hard for you, all of this… Abraham gone and having a *boppli* without a man by your side."

It was at that moment the realization hit Hannah that she was in this alone. Her husband had been snatched away from her and the only man she loved couldn't have loved her like she had thought if he was looking for love elsewhere. The tears came back.

"Sorry, Hannah. Was it something I said?"

Hannah shook her head and cried harder. Embarrassed to be crying in front of him, she placed both hands over her face and sobbed. Soon she felt arms around her and she hugged him back and cried into his shoulder as he patted her on the back in a comforting manner.

"Everything will be okay, Hannah. I'll see to it." He held her tight.

"Well, well. Isn't this a cozy scene?"

The two of them jumped apart and looked over to see Lizzy silhouetted in the doorway of the barn.

Lizzy said, "I can see now why you wanted me to tell him about Joel, Hannah. It was so you could have him all to yourself. I bet you couldn't wait for your husband to die so you could be with him."

"Lizzy!" Levi said.

Hannah took a step forward. "This isn't what it looks like. I was just upset and Levi was comforting me."

"Ever heard 'judge not lest ye be judged?' The two of you were quick about judging me over Joel and now I find you cozying up to each other." She put her hands on her hips and looked at Hannah. "You should be ashamed of yourself, Hannah. Your husband has only just been buried. And you, Levi, we've only just ended things between us. You both disgust me. I wonder what the bishop will say about the pair of you." She turned and stomped away.

Hannah wiped her eyes and giggled, seeing the funny side. But Levi wasn't laughing.

"I'm sorry," Hannah said. "Every time bad things happen I see the funny side of them."

Gradually, his face broke into a smile. "It is a little funny when you think about it."

"It is, isn't it?"

They both laughed and Hannah wiped the moisture left over from her tears, drying her cheeks. When they walked out of the barn, they saw Lizzy walking out of the house with one small bag tucked under her arm.

"Where are you going, Lizzy? It's nearly dinner time."

"I'm leaving. You were probably sweet on him all along," she said nodding to Levi.

"You've got this all wrong, Lizzy."

"We're only friends," Levi added. "Hannah and I have only ever been friends."

That was the last thing Hannah wanted to hear. Lizzy ignored both of them and kept walking.

"Where is she going?" Levi asked.

"My best guess is she's going next door to the Beatties. She got along with them really well."

"I should leave you in peace, Hannah."

"I'm sad that you're not getting married now. But as you said, this is good to find out before you married—that you're not suited."

"I know. I'm sorry this all happened at your *haus*. You don't need all this around you. You need to have peace around you. I hope she doesn't say anything to the bishop."

"I don't think she will, considering she'd have to tell him she neglected to tell Joel about your engagement when they went out this morning."

Levi smiled and nodded. "It was the quickest engagement ever."

"I don't think Lizzy will be back."

He gave her a nod. "I'll leave you in peace. Bye, Hannah."

"Goodbye, Levi."

When Hannah walked back into the house, she was secretly pleased she was by herself again.

CHAPTER 17

Hannah hadn't seen a single person all day and she had no idea what was going on with Lizzy, but at least she'd had time to answer all the letters of condolences for her husband's death. She hadn't been able to get out of her mind how it felt to have Levi's arms around her. Whenever she had a moment of feeling alone, she would close her eyes and pretend she was back in his warm embrace.

She happened to look out the kitchen window just in time to see Miriam's buggy heading to the house, and she met her at the door.

"It's nice to see you! Come in."

"You'll never guess what happened," Miriam said as she hurried through the door.

"What? Do I have to sit down?"

Miriam giggled. "Probably."

When Hannah was seated in the living room,

Miriam took a deep breath and began. "Joel and Lizzy are getting married."

Hannah slapped her hand over her mouth in shock. "*Nee!* I don't believe it. It's only been a day or two. They've only known each other two days."

"*Jah!*"

"How did that happen so fast?"

"I heard from Levi that she left your house and went to the Beatties.'"

"That's right. We guessed that she was heading to their *haus* right after she and Levi ended things. I can't believe the bishop has allowed this. He usually cautions young people who end one relationship to wait awhile before they start another."

Miriam shrugged.

"I can only imagine how poor Levi feels."

"Well, what happened was that the Beattie's moved back into the main *haus* from the *grossdaddi haus* so that Lizzy could stay with them, and Joel moved into the *grossdaddi haus* by himself."

"That's a big upheaval for them, since they'd only just moved in."

"I know."

"How is Levi?" Hannah asked.

"Worried about you more than anything. I told him I'd come to check on you."

"You're the first person I've seen today."

"Blackie's still lame?"

"Levi said he's coming back after work to check on

him. Do you mind if you walk him up and down while I watch and see if he's still limping?"

"Okay, but let's have some hot tea first," Miriam said.

"Sounds like a good idea."

They both moved into the kitchen.

"I can't believe that she's getting married so quickly to Joel. Does Levi feel awful?"

"*Jah*, pretty much. I think he mostly feels a little foolish. Especially since it all happen in front of you."

"He shouldn't let that worry him."

"Well, it wasn't an ideal situation for him."

"It wouldn't be good for anybody. He brought her out here and then she's set to marry someone else in a matter of days."

Hannah didn't say so, but she was glad that she was by herself now and living in peace rather than having Lizzy stay with her. It was such a relief, and it made being alone peaceful rather than lonely.

"So, has Levi talked to the bishop? I guess he has."

"*Jah*. Levi went to the bishop's house last night. Joel went there after to tell him he wanted to marry Lizzy."

"Joel's a sensible man even though he's young. They must really have gotten along well together. I just can't see him rushing into anything," Hannah said. "Well, I couldn't until this happened."

"Unless he's on the rebound. He was about to get married to somebody else remember?"

"That's right."

Hannah thought back to her own rebound situation when she was so devastated about Matthew Miller it was easy to fall into the arms of Abraham. Especially when her parents were pushing him at her. "Rebounds are never good. We'll have to hope this one is the exception," Hannah said.

Miriam nodded while she filled up the teakettle with water.

"I wish this had never happened to Levi. He's such a good man and I hate to see him be disappointed like this," Hannah said.

"Disappointment is a part of life sometimes."

"You've got that right. It sure seems to be."

"We've each had our share," Miriam said.

Hannah knew that Miriam was talking about the fact that she still didn't have a child after many years of marriage. That was Miriam's disappointment. And Hannah's disappointment was that she never married Levi.

"It's all hard to believe somehow," Hannah said.

"I shouldn't say it, but I'm glad that things didn't work out with Levi and Lizzy. Is that awful?" Miriam asked.

"You're being honest."

"*Jah,* I think that you and Levi are far better suited."

Hannah giggled. "Don't be silly."

"I mean it."

"If Levi and I had been meant for each other we would've gotten together years ago."

"And perhaps you should've."

"Ah, but we didn't," Hannah said.

Miriam laughed. "We could go back and forth like this for hours. Who knows what the future holds?"

"I suppose only *Gott* knows and we just have to hope for the best."

"And pray," Miriam pointed out.

"*Jah*, and especially pray."

"How about I take you out for lunch? I think we could both do with some cheering up."

"And lunch will do that?" Hannah asked.

"Absolutely. Especially if it's followed by dessert."

Hannah laughed. "I like the sound of that. I've been very hungry lately."

"Good. I'll take the kettle off the stove and we'll make our escape."

Hannah stood up. "Let's do it. I'll let Blackie wait for Levi."

CHAPTER 18

Hannah and Miriam had a lovely day out together and Hannah tried her best to put all the problems behind her.

She walked into the house. It felt odd being in the house without Abraham, having never lived there without him. Hannah slumped down onto the couch, pleased that she wasn't hungry after such a big lunch. Since no one was staying with her, she could just have a piece of fruit or cheese or something for dinner if she felt hungry later.

It was silly to have those crazy thoughts about Levi that she'd had the last few days. God was surely showing her that it was a bad idea. It was God who had charge over the rest of her life, she told herself. What was most important was her child, and she was determined to give her child the very best life that she could.

She put her hand over her stomach and for the first

time she thought she felt the baby move. Were those tiny flutters really her baby moving about? She stayed still and felt them again. It was the first sign of life, and her heart was filled with an extra surge of love.

"Hello, my *boppli*. I can't wait to hold you in my arms."

"Hello," a male voice called out, startling her.

She opened the door to see Levi and her heart beat faster. Was he there to tell her he'd always been in love with her and couldn't go on another day until he knew whether she felt the same? "Hello. I didn't hear your buggy."

"I'm here to check on Blackie."

"I put him back in the house paddock. I was going to move him back into the stable later."

"Okay. I'll get a lead." Levi headed to the barn.

Hannah walked out of the house, glad that he'd stopped by. As she watched him striding into the barn she imagined that they were married. They'd always gotten along so well and they understood each other completely.

Levi came out of the barn.

"I can see you need some new leathers."

"Do I?"

"You do. They're practically worn through."

"Thanks for letting me know."

Together they walked to get Blackie.

"As soon as Blackie is better, come into the store

with him and I'll replace what needs to be replaced on his harness at no charge."

"Now, Levi, I can pay for it. I'm not destitute or anything. Abraham left me with —"

"It's my gift to you, not because I think you're destitute." He gave a little chuckle.

"Well, *denke.* That's very kind. I'm glad you spotted it because I wouldn't have noticed until something broke. Abraham used to look after all that kind of thing."

"You're welcome." He opened the gate and they both walked through. Blackie stopped eating grass and looked up at them, and started walking toward them.

"He looks alright to me."

"Yes, he does today."

Levi slipped the halter over his head and led him up the paddock for Hannah to watch.

"He seems fine," Hannah said. "I'll walk him now, and you see what you think."

Levi handed the lead to her and then she walked quickly up the paddock, breaking out into a little run.

"Don't exert yourself, Hannah."

"I won't."

"Yes, he looks fine." Levi walked over and picked up one of Blackie's legs to check his hoof. He worked his way around the horse until he had looked at each hoof. "I don't think there are any concerns. It's time to call the blacksmith about getting his new shoes put on. Best leave him a day or two after that before you drive him again, just to be safe. Do you have to go anywhere?"

"No, but I was thinking of going to go into the markets to see if they had any kittens for sale. Sometimes they do, and I was just going to go on the off chance."

"I can take you."

"I can't take up all your time."

"I've already organized people to look after the workshop today, thinking I'd be spending the time with someone else. I can't think of anything I'd rather do than have a look for a kitten with you."

"Kittens," Hannah corrected. "I'd like two."

"I'm ready when you are."

"*Denke,* Levi. I'm glad you came when you did."

After they put the horse back in his stall, they headed toward the markets.

On the way there, he asked, "Are these going to be house cats or barn cats?"

"House cats. I've always wanted to have cats, but Abraham was allergic."

They kept the conversation away from Joel and Lizzy, and as they drove Hannah pretended they were a married couple on their weekly visit to the markets.

Together they walked into the farmers market, and right under an awning at the front there was a young girl of around twelve sitting with a basket of kittens. The hand drawn sign said, "To give away, free to a good home."

Hannah was delighted and she looked at Levi. "*Denke* for bringing me here, this is perfect timing."

He chuckled. "Let's hope she has two left," he said.

They walked over and asked about the kittens.

"I had six. I wanted to keep them but my mother won't let me. We didn't mean for our cat to have these kittens. We took her to the vet to be fixed and he told us she was already having kittens."

"How many are in there?" Hannah asked, as the girl hadn't opened the basket yet.

"There are four left," she said. "You could have two each."

Levi chuckled. "You're a good salesperson."

The young girl smiled as she proudly opened the basket.

Hannah crouched down. "Oh look at them! They are so tiny. How old are they?"

"They're eight weeks old. Our cat had six kittens, and the other two were black, but I gave them away this morning."

Hannah looked up at Levi, "Which ones do you like? The tabbies or the calicos?" There were two of each.

"I don't know. I like them all the same. It's your decision."

"How many do you want?" The young girl asked.

"Two," Hannah and Levi answered at the same time.

"I think I like the two tabbies," Hannah said.

"Which ones are the boys and which ones the girls?" Levi asked.

The girl started picking the cats up and turning them upside down. "I can't tell. But calico cats are almost always females."

"I guess it doesn't matter. I'm not going to breed from them or anything. As soon as they're old enough I'll take them to the vet to get fixed."

"Don't leave it too long," the young girl said.

Hannah laughed. "I definitely won't!"

"The tabbies?" Levi asked.

Hannah nodded and looked back at the young girl. "Is it okay if I take the two tabbies?"

"Sure. You look like you would look after them."

"They'll have a very good home. You stay here," Levi said. "I'll see if I can get a cardboard box."

"You can get one at the food store," the young girl called after him.

When he was gone the young girl informed Hannah that the kittens hadn't had any of their shots yet.

Hannah assured her that she would take them to the vet and made sure they got everything they needed, and that made the young girl smile.

Soon they were heading back home and Hannah was delighted. She was holding the kittens on her knees in a cardboard box.

"You look pretty happy, Hannah. I haven't seen you like that in a while."

"I've wanted cats for such a long time."

"You should have whatever makes you happy."

"*Denke*, Levi. And what can we do to make you happy?"

"Spending time with you makes me happy, Hannah." He glanced over at her and she looked away feeling a little embarrassed. "I'm sorry. I shouldn't have said that."

"No, that's okay. I like spending time with you too."

He smiled. "Now, do you have everything you need for the cats?"

"I do. I've been thinking about them for awhile, so I've got everything ready. I've got old saucers that I've kept to use for food bowls and a large water bowl, cat trays and a large basket they can sleep in. I'll fill it with a warm blanket."

When the buggy stopped at the house, Hannah said, "Are you coming inside to watch the kittens?"

"Okay. I'll carry the box in for you."

As soon as Hannah let the kittens out in the living room, they sniffed around. "I think I'll leave them in the kitchen at first, so they get to know one space before they explore another."

"Good idea. And leave the box on its side for them to get into. They might like something familiar for a few days."

Soon the cats were hiding back in their box on the kitchen floor, curled up with a woolen blanket.

"They certainly like it in there. They prefer the box to the basket."

"They feel protected," Hannah said. "Would you like a hot tea, or anything?"

"*Nee, denke.* I should go. I had a nice time today."

"Me too."

He turned and walked out of the kitchen and she followed.

When he got to the door he turned around to face her. "I'll be back tomorrow to check on Blackie. Do you want me to call the blacksmith?"

"*Jah.* I'd appreciate that. Bye, Levi."

"Bye, Hannah."

Hannah closed the door and then moved to the living room to look out the window at him. She was a little disappointed that he didn't take their admissions of liking each other further, since it had taken a huge amount of courage for her to admit she liked him as well. Or, had he just meant he liked her as a friend?

CHAPTER 19

Levi drove away from the house glad that he had let Hannah know his true feelings toward her. But, had she taken that to mean that he liked her as merely a friend? It was too soon after Abraham's death to ask her on a date. Then again, he reminded himself he'd thought it too soon after Matthew Miller left the community to ask her out, and then the next thing he heard she was engaged to Abraham.

He pulled back on the reins and moved his buggy off the road. What if the same thing happened again? Just telling her that spending time with her made him happy wasn't expressing the true extent of the love that he held for her. He looked back over his shoulder at her house and wondered whether he should go back and tell her that he loved her.

"There's no one she'd marry," he said to himself.

"Then again, I didn't imagine that she'd marry Abraham." Could he risk losing their friendship if he laid it on the line how he felt and she didn't feel the same? He decided that he couldn't tell her how he felt at this time. She was having a baby and her husband had only just died. At this time of her life what she needed more than anything was for him to be a friend.

Putting aside his desire to be with the woman he loved, he clicked his horse onward.

~

HANNAH WENT to bed that night pleased that she finally had her kittens. She'd played with them for hours before they'd worn themselves out. She'd made toys for them by tying pieces of rags on strings and pulling them along the floor while the kittens ran after them.

While Hannah tried to sleep, she tossed and turned, trying to push Levi out of her mind. If he loved her, he wouldn't have gotten engaged to Lizzy. That was a fact and she had to face it no matter how much she hoped it wasn't the case.

~

THE VERY NEXT day Levi looked at Blackie and said he was fine. He told her the blacksmith would be there in the afternoon. Levi then asked her, if the blacksmith said Blackie was okay to go the distance, to bring the buggy into the workshop soon to get new leathers.

THE NEXT DAY, as she hitched Blackie to go to Levi's workshop, she realized how everything was so much easier with a man around. She had taken it for granted exactly how much Abraham had done around the place.

Just as she had taken hold of Blackie to back him into the harness, she caught sight of a familiar buggy coming to the house. It was either the bishop or Ruth. She patted Blackie on his neck. "Wait here, boy." She secured him and then walked away from the barn to meet the buggy.

When it drew closer she saw that it was Ruth, by herself.

"On your way out, are you, Hannah?"

"I was just going to Levi's workshop. He's going to replace some of the harness leathers for me. I don't have to be there at any particular time. Come inside and I'll fix us some tea."

"Are you certain?"

"*Jah,* of course. Come in."

Ruth followed Hannah inside and sat down at the kitchen table.

"How are you coping by yourself, Hannah?"

Hannah placed the kettle on the stove. "Very well. Everything's fine. I was just thinking this morning, though, how everything is easier with a man around."

"Perhaps you'll get married again."

"One day, maybe," Hannah said as she sat opposite Ruth.

"You're still young."

Hannah got up from the table. "I'll get us some cookies."

"*Denke.*"

"I do have a lot of help from Miriam and from Stephen. They're always watching over me."

"*Gut.*"

The kittens came out of their box.

"Oh, these are my kittens. I only just got them and I haven't named them yet." When Ruth didn't look too impressed to see the kittens, Hannah shut them in another room.

"It was a surprise about Lizzy and Joel," Ruth said.

"*Jah*, it was."

"I thought it would've been good that the two of you be here together until her wedding, but she said you didn't get along."

"*Jah*, that's true. We had a few tense moments. Excuse me, I'll just wash my hands before I fix the tea." Hannah slipped into the next room to wash her hands where she had a basin, soap, and a hand towel. She hoped to change the topic away from Lizzy, Levi and Joel.

When she walked back into the kitchen and started fixing the tea, Ruth said, "Next week there'll be a single man staying with us and I thought we might invite you for dinner while he's here."

Hannah stopped pouring the hot water. "Oh, no. I'm not ready for that kind of thing. Not yet."

Ruth giggled. "It doesn't hurt to ask. You just said yourself that things are easier with a man around."

Hannah continued making the tea and when she passed a cup to Ruth and sat down with one herself, she gave what Ruth had said a little more thought. "And where does this man live?"

"He's from Harts County."

"That's where Lizzy was from originally."

"*Jah*, I know." Ruth sipped her tea. "I didn't know whether to raise the subject of his visit with you. I hope I didn't upset you. Some people heal faster than others."

"Wouldn't people talk if I was suddenly keeping company with a man so soon?"

"Most likely." Ruth chuckled. "I wouldn't let what anyone says bother you. You wouldn't be doing anything wrong."

"I just want to do what's right. I've only just answered all the letters that people sent me. Most of them were from Abraham's relations. I mean, what would they think?"

"Hmm. You're giving this a lot of serious thought."

"Oh, well, not really."

Ruth leaned forward. "Have you been thinking about one man in particular?"

Hannah gulped. She couldn't lie and neither did she want to admit thinking about another man so soon after Abraham was gone. "I can't answer you, Ruth."

"That says a lot."

Hannah breathed out heavily.

"I shouldn't pry. Forget I said anything. You'll know when the time is right for you. Now, how's your *boppli?*"

"I've been seeing the midwife regularly. She said all is well."

"I'm glad to hear it."

An hour later, Ruth left and Hannah finished hitching the buggy and made her way to Levi's workshop.

When she got there she saw exactly how busy he was. He was on the phone when she arrived, and no sooner had he hung up then it rang again. She could see through to his workshop from the small office where she was, and there were two workers using various industrial sewing machines, and she guessed the other machines were to cut the leather.

He looked up from his desk, "I'm sorry, Hannah. The place has gone crazy today. I'll let the phone go to message and I'll take a look at the harness."

Once they were outside, he measured the harness and made some notes. "We've got all that you need in stock, I'm sure. Why don't you have a seat inside and I'll have this replaced for you in no time."

"Okay."

Soon Hannah was on her way home with a brand new harness. Levi had agreed to come to dinner that night as her way of saying a small thank you. On her way home, she stopped by Miriam and Stephen's house and invited them as well. Talk would surely get around if anyone found out that she and Levi had been having dinner alone at her house.

CHAPTER 20

It was two months later and Hannah was at the wedding of Lizzy and Joel. Very few people in the community knew that Lizzy had originally come there to marry Levi. Hannah and Miriam had certainly told no one, and the bishop and his wife would not have liked things like that to get around.

Lizzy had only spoken to Hannah briefly at the Sunday meetings and their relationship was still strained, although both of them were making an effort. Hannah still had many bags of Lizzy's possessions in the spare room; Lizzy had never come back to collect them. Hannah never mentioned it, figuring Lizzy would be back sooner or later.

Levi was noticeably absent from the wedding and both Hannah and Miriam were concerned for him.

When the reception was over and they were having

the meal after the wedding, Miriam said, "I don't blame him for not coming. If this had happened to me I wouldn't go to the wedding either."

"I guess I would feel the same way."

"It's ruined his confidence with women."

"Do you think he'll be alone forever?" Hannah asked.

"I hope not. I would like to have some nieces and nephews here, without having to travel to Ohio."

"You'll have your own soon," Hannah said hoping she wasn't bringing up a sore topic.

"I certainly hope so, but it's easier for me if I don't think about it."

"Of course. I'm sorry for bringing it up."

"Don't be. It's something I have to deal with."

"We can share my *boppli*," Hannah said.

Miriam laughed. "Don't you worry about that. I'll be a second *mudder* to your *boppli* whether you like it or not."

"My child will be very blessed to have you around."

"Your child might be the closest I get to having one of my own. And now I have to go and help the ladies in the kitchen."

"Okay, I'll just sit here and watch everyone enjoying themselves."

HANNAH HAD SLEPT IN, and now she hurried to get dressed when she knew that Levi would be there for his usual Saturday morning visit. On Saturday mornings, he came to see if she was okay and to do whatever jobs had surfaced during the week. This time there were no jobs for him to do but she would enjoy the morning cup of tea.

Hoping she had enough time, she had a quick shower. As soon as she turned the water off she heard a buggy. She dried herself off and pulled on her clean clothes and set a prayer *kapp* over her already pinned hair.

When he knocked on the door, she yelled out that she was coming. She walked down the stairs telling herself not to rush and she stepped carefully. Just as she was on the second-to-last step, the two cats rushed beneath her feet and she had to take a giant step to avoid them. She took a tumble and fell hard onto the floor.

Levi rushed through the door and saw her on the floor. "Hannah, what happened?"

"I tripped on the cats."

He knelt down and helped her move to sit on the bottom step. "Are you okay? Are you hurt anywhere?" He stood back up.

"I think I jarred my ankle or something."

"Wiggle your toes."

She looked down and was able to wiggle them.

"I think that means nothing's broken at least. You fell hard; I heard it from outside. I'm taking you to the hospital."

Hannah stood and held onto his shoulders for

balance. "*Nee*. I'm fine. I just need to sit down for a while longer."

He helped her to the couch. "You sit down, and I'll call a taxi and take you to the hospital to get checked over."

"I'm sure that's not necessary."

"You can't be too careful."

While he was calling a taxi, Hannah put her hands over her face. If something happened to her baby she'd never forgive herself.

Minutes later, Levi came back into the room. "How are you feeling now?"

She wiped her eyes and then he saw that she was crying. Levi quickly sat beside her and put his arm around her. "Don't be upset."

"What about the *boppli?* What if—"

"Everything's going to be okay."

"You don't know that; you can't say for certain."

"Let us pray." He took hold of both her hands and prayed for the safety of her baby and for her health. When they opened their eyes, he said, "I don't think the taxi will be long. I told them to be quick because we have to take someone to the hospital."

"*Gut, denke*. Where are the cats?"

He smiled and said, "Don't worry about the cats."

"I think I managed to avoid them."

He shook his head.

"I was so careful going down the steps and at the last minute they ran underneath my feet."

"Well, that's what cats do."

When the taxi pulled up, he helped her to her feet, wrapped her in a shawl and helped her get in the backseat of the taxi. He went around and got in beside her.

On the way there, Hannah said, "I'm starting to worry about the baby. I haven't felt any movement or kicks since the fall."

When Levi didn't say anything encouraging, she felt quite worried.

"We just have to trust, Hannah," he finally said.

Hannah nodded and prayed the rest of the way.

Levi had called ahead and the hospital staff were expecting her. They were alarmed when he'd told them she was pregnant.

They arrived at the hospital and Hannah was whisked away, while they directed him to fill out paperwork.

When he was finished, he asked the receptionist where he should go. He was told she was having an ultrasound and was directed to the emergency department, where he sat and waited.

It was a chore for him to push negative thoughts out of his mind while he sat there. Half an hour later, a man in a white coat came into the room. He appeared to be a doctor. His eyes fixed upon Levi as he strode toward him.

"Are you Mr. Fisher?" For all intents and purposes, he was looking after her, so he'd taken on the role of husband. He nodded. "Have you been looking after my wife?"

CHAPTER 21

The doctor met his eyes and then smiled. "Yes, and your wife and the baby are fine. You can go in and see her now."

Levi leaped up and shook the doctor's hand. "Thank you, Doctor, thank you."

Levi was shown into a room with three empty beds, and there was a nurse next to Hannah's bed writing something on her chart.

"Here's your husband now," the nurse said.

Levi walked over to Hannah and grabbed her hand.

"I'm all right, Levi and so is the baby."

He nodded, not trusting his voice for the moment.

When the nurse left, Hannah said, "Did you hear what the nurse said?"

He smiled, and nodded again as he let go of her hand.

Hannah said, "I'm sorry about that. They assume you're my husband because you brought me in."

"I'm not sorry." He shook his head and moved closer to her. "Hannah, I'd like to be your husband and I know the timing is wrong and if I waited for the right timing I might be waiting forever. Hannah, I would be the happiest man in the world if you say you'll marry me. If you say no, we'll forget what I just said." He gave a nervous laugh.

"You want to marry me?"

He picked up her hand. "I do."

"I can't believe it."

He looked away from her. "I'm sorry. Forget I said anything."

"I don't want to forget."

"Really? Wait... then you ..." When he saw her smiling face he knew she felt the same. "Years ago, I was just about to ask you on a buggy ride and I tried to pluck up the courage, and the next thing I knew I saw you with the Miller boy."

"I grew impatient while waiting for you. I should have told him no."

"You had feelings for me back then?" he asked.

"I did, but I was foolish and impatient. I should've waited."

He was pleased with how things were going, so he continued, "And then when Matthew left, you were so upset about him and I wanted your full attention so I waited again. And then…"

"And then I married Abraham."

"*Jah.* Hannah, I've loved you forever, and I had to try to forget about you."

"Shh. It doesn't matter now."

"*Jah,* it does. I need to confess some things to you. It was selfish of me that I fell to a new low when I heard you were having a baby. Please forgive me for my selfishness. I wasn't thinking of the joy that the child would bring you and Abraham. It somehow made you feel even further away from me. That's why I had to get away and I visited my brother. Andrew saw my pain and that's when he suggested I marry and invited Lizzy to the house. A day after I got engaged to Lizzy, I found out Abraham had died." He looked down and shook his head. "I was torn. I didn't want to be engaged to Lizzy, I admit that now. It seems the timing was wrong every step of the way."

"So you didn't know Abraham had died when you proposed to Lizzy?"

"That's right." He shook his head again. "I don't mean it to sound like I was ready to pounce on a man's wife as soon as he died."

"I know that's not what you're trying to do."

"Asking Lizzy to marry me made sense at the time. I have so many regrets. I could never shake you from my mind—never."

"I didn't know. I thought you weren't interested in me, and my parents were pushing me to marry Abraham and I thought why not? I was so low at that time, I thought marrying would make things all better."

He laughed. "So we've just admitted a few things to each other. Will you marry me, Hannah? It doesn't have to be right away, I can wait."

She looked into his eyes and put her hand over her tummy. "I come with a *boppli,* and two cats who run up walls and do crazy things and scratch the couches."

"And I come with myself and a business where I work a lot. Do you think we could make this work?"

She nodded. "I think so."

"Does that mean you're saying yes?"

"Jah."

He laughed. "I can't believe it's taken us all this time. We could've been together years ago."

"Jah, all this time to get it right."

He looked around and then said, "Are you ready to go home?"

"They want to check the baby again in another couple of hours. You can go and I'll get a taxi later."

He held her hand tighter. "I'm not leaving your side."

Hannah was two months away from having the baby when she and Levi got married. From the wedding they were moving into Levi's home and they would begin their new life together there. Everyone in the community seemed pleased about it and there were no whispers circulating about it being too soon after Abraham's passing. Hannah's baby would have a father and the long-term bachelor, Levi, would be married.

The wedding took place at Miriam's newly renovated house. Hannah sat at the wedding table with Levi, finally feeling that her life made sense. Even though she'd made choices in the past that weren't right for her, in the end it had all worked out. She never thought for a moment that she would marry for the second time in her life when she'd been this young.

Levi put his head close to hers. "I never thought I could be so happy."

"I hope I'll keep making you happy."

He smiled. "You always have."

They'd talked about having many children and the life they'd share together.

In usual late pregnancy fashion, Hannah had to excuse herself to go to the restroom. On the way she was confronted with Lizzy.

"I knew you wanted him, Hannah."

"Well, you knew more than I did, then."

"Anyway, it worked out well for both of us. I'm married to Joel and I'm happy, and you look happy with Levi. Hannah, do you think we ever might be friends?"

"I'd like that." Hannah saw no reason why they couldn't be polite to one another and eventually they might even enjoy each other's company.

"Good. I'll make the effort to be friends with you.

That will make Joel happy. And then we can have you and Levi to dinner."

"I look forward to it."

"Thank you, Hannah. I'm glad we had this talk."

"Me too." After they exchanged smiles Hannah continued to the ladies room.

After she came out from the bathroom, she poked her head in the kitchen to see ladies busily rushing about.

"Go back out and enjoy yourself, Hannah," Miriam had just come up behind her.

"I'm just having a peek to see what's happening."

"Come on." Miriam slipped her arm through hers and took her back out to the table where Levi was waiting. "There. Sit down with your husband, *schweschder*-in-law." Miriam gave a little laugh.

CHAPTER 22

It was two months later, and Hannah was two days over her due date. Levi had taken time off from work so he could be there with her.

He made her breakfast and had her sit down on the couch while he brought it to her.

"I'm not an invalid, you know. I can still do things."

"You don't need to do anything, that's why I've taken time off."

Hannah didn't mention it to Levi, but all night she'd had slight twinges of tightening across the stomach but they weren't painful so she didn't mention it. "I think I should go to see the midwife today."

"*Nee*, she'll come to you. I'll call her." He took a swallow of coffee and placed his cup down. "Do you think the *boppli's* close?"

She hoped so, since she was past her due date. "I just want her to check me over. Maybe the bumpy buggy ride will bring on the labor. I've heard of that happening and I just want this baby out."

"I'm not going to argue with a woman's instinct. When do you want to go?"

"Soon."

Levi finished another mouthful of coffee. "I'll hitch the buggy and call her and tell her we're coming." He leaned over and kissed her on the forehead and walked out.

A minute after Levi was gone, she felt something that she had no doubt was a contraction. Things were getting painful and she was still in her nightgown. Wanting to get dressed, she stood up and then her water broke. Shocked, she stood there staring at her wet nightgown and the puddle of water on the floor.

This was happening, and happening in a few hours. Her long awaited baby would soon be in her arms. "Levi!"

He came running back. "What is it?"

"My water just broke."

A look of fear washed over his face. "I'll call her back."

Hannah didn't know what to do until the midwife got there, but she remembered that walking around brought labor on quicker. She'd waited nine months for this baby and didn't want to wait any longer than she had to. She paced up and down until Levi came running back into the house.

"How are you feeling?"

"I don't know."

"I'll get you a dry nightgown." He ran up the stairs, taking them two at a time. When he got back he said, "You should come upstairs now if you want to give birth in the bedroom."

She shook her head. "I don't know what I want." Hannah changed gowns, and kept pacing up and down until the midwife arrived.

THREE HOURS LATER, Hannah was propped up in bed and holding her baby in her arms while Levi, Miriam, and the midwife looked on.

"We have a *dochder*. Levi, we have a *dochder*."

Levi wiped the tears from his eyes. "It's unbelievable."

"Do you want to hold her?"

"Of course." He leaned down and carefully took the bundle into his arms. He looked down at the tiny pink face with the perfect features. "She's even got small eyelashes and everything. She's *wunderbaar*."

"Have you chosen a name yet?" Miriam asked.

"We always said if it turned out to be a girl, we'd call her April because she was to be born in April."

"Only just a day later and we would've had to call her May," Levi pointed out with a laugh.

"April is a beautiful name," Miriam said. "I'm sure Tricia and Andrew will visit soon to see her."

Levi said, "I was disappointed that they couldn't make it to the wedding." He looked at Miriam. "Here, Auntie, have a hold."

Her face lighted up as she took the baby and held her close against her.

HANNAH LOOKED at each person in the room and was grateful. She thanked God that her life was turned around. It had taken her and Levi a long time to be married to each other and they'd made many mistakes in between times, but now they were together and deliciously happy. Things could've turned out very differently. She reminded herself not to push April into a relationship when she got older, and she determined to allow her to follow her heart. And she'd warn April that the decisions she made in her youth were vital to the happiness of the rest of her life—no one had thought to tell Hannah that.

WHEN LEVI and Hannah were alone that night, Hannah said, "I hope I'll be a good *mudder*."

"You'll be the best." Levi peeped in at baby April who was in their room in her crib.

"Levi, we very nearly didn't marry at all."

He sat on the bed next to her. "I know. We have to be grateful that everything turned out well for us."

"I am, but I feel bad that Abraham had to die for us to be together."

He picked up her hand and held it. "Shh. Don't think of things like that. You made him happy in his last years, that's what you should focus on. We live in the present, we learn from the past, and we must be mindful of the future."

"I hope I made him happy. Anyway, when did you get so wise?"

He laughed. "As soon as April came into the world, so about six hours ago. I'm a *daed* now. I have to be wise." He leaned over and kissed Hannah on her forehead. "I'll feed the cats and then I'll come to bed. Do you need anything from downstairs?"

"*Nee.*"

When he walked out of the room Hannah wondered if it was possible that her future could be better. Levi had brought so much happiness into her life, and now there was April. She had a proper family and there was no effort that had to be applied to her marriage—it was effortless to get along with Levi. She closed her eyes and thanked God for finally bringing Levi to her.

∽

TWO YEARS ON, Hannah and Levi were expecting their second child while Miriam and Stephen were delighted to finally be expecting their first. Miriam and

Hannah were pleased their children would be the same ages to play together just as they'd done as children.

WHAT BECAME OF LIZZY? Lizzy had found it hard to get along with everyone in the community in Lancaster County, and had talked Joel and his parents into moving to Harts County. In her letters to Hannah, Lizzy said they were all much happier there. Hannah hoped so.

Thank you for reading Amish Widow's Story.

www.SamanthaPriceAuthor.com

THE NEXT BOOK IN THE SERIES

Book 15

Amish Widow's Decision

After Faye's husband was murdered, there was little time to mourn since she had to take over her late husband's business.

Everyone told her a woman couldn't be successful, especially an Amish woman. She was determined to prove them all wrong.

Soon, Faye is in fear for her life when she becomes a suspect in her late husband's murder. Someone's out to get her. When she finds out she's pregnant, she has more reason to keep out of harm's way. Soon, everyone she comes in contact with falls under suspicion.

EXPECTANT AMISH WIDOWS

Book 1 Amish Widow's Hope

Book 2 The Pregnant Amish Widow

Book 3 Amish Widow's Faith

Book 4 Their Son's Amish Baby

Book 5 Amish Widow's Proposal

Book 6 The Pregnant Amish Nanny

Book 7 A Pregnant Widow's Amish Vacation

Book 8 The Amish Firefighter's Widow

Book 9 Amish Widow's Secret

Book 10 The Middle-Aged Amish Widow

Book 11 Amish Widow's Escape

Book 12 Amish Widow's Christmas

Book 13 Amish Widow's New Hope

Book 14 Amish Widow's Story

Book 15 Amish Widow's Decision

Book 16 Amish Widow's Trust

Book 17 The Amish Potato Farmer's Widow

Book 18 Amish Widow's Tears

Book 19 Amish Widow's Heart

ALL SAMANTHA PRICE'S BOOK SERIES

Amish Maids Trilogy

Amish Love Blooms

Amish Misfits

The Amish Bonnet Sisters

Amish Women of Pleasant Valley

Ettie Smith Amish Mysteries

Amish Secret Widows' Society

Expectant Amish Widows

Seven Amish Bachelors

ALL SAMANTHA PRICE'S BOOK SERIES

Amish Foster Girls

Amish Brides

Amish Romance Secrets

Amish Twin Hearts

Amish Wedding Season

Gretel Koch Jewel Thief

Made in the USA
Monee, IL
31 October 2023

45519332R00100